THE TRUTH IN THE BONES

THE CONISBOROUGH CHRONICLES (BOOK 2)

MICK FENLON

This is a work of fiction. All locations contained within this work exist. All characters and events however, are entirely the results of the authors imagination. Any resemblance to actual people and events is entirely coincidental.

This book is dedicated to the memories of two dear friends who sadly passed away during its writing.

Pete Thorpe and Gerald `Cheesie' Clayton Rest in Peace boys. It was an honour and a pleasure to have known you both.

Contents

PART ONE

1982

Chapter 1

Monday 19th July 1982

Minneymoor Field, Conisborough.

`Look at this one, she's got it in her mouth!' fifteen years old Lee Jennings said excitedly to the small gathering of young boys.

`That's nowt.' Said his twin brother Carl. `This dirty cow'

`She's got one in her mouth an' one up her fanny an' all!'

`Fuck me yeah! Looks like she's enjoying it an' all the slag.' Lee said.

`Give us a look then.' Said eleven years old Simon West.

`No way, we can't do that. You two aren't old enough to look at this sort o' stuff, yer wouldn't understand it.' Carl said.

`Course we would, he's eleven an' I'm twelve, we're not babies.' Chris Hughes whined. `An' anyway, you two are only fifteen. It's not like you're grown-ups or owt.' He added.

`At least we know what it's all about though. What do you pair o' retards know about shagging?' Lee countered.

`Yer get a bird an' yer both get undressed an' then when yer dick gets hard yer stick it in her an' shag her until yer need to piss an' then yer piss inside her an' that makes her piss as well. If yer don't want to get her pregnant yer wear a rubber Johnny an' that catches yer piss.' Simon said matter of factly.

The two older boys burst into hysterics at this, clinging on to one another as they laughed uncontrollably.

`See, I told yer. Yer don't know owt about shagging. Yer don't piss in a bird when yer give her one.' Carl said a few moments later. ``Yer *come* in her.'

`The technical terms spunk up in her.' His brother added.

`I know, that's what I meant.' Simon said, embarrassed now.

`No yer dint, I bet you've never even spunked up yet. Bet yer ant got a clue what we're on about.'

`Give em a quick look Lee, it's worth it for laugh he's just give us an' yer never know, he might get his first wet dream tonight.'

`Go on then. Five minutes an' then we put em back.' He said handing over the two pornographic magazines to the younger boys.

The four boys had been playing cricket on the Minneymoor Field since just after four o'clock that afternoon. About an hour previously they had tired of the game with there being such a small number of them and had decided to try `Kick Can Tommy' instead. It was whilst hiding behind the Elephant Rock that Simon had discovered the magazines tucked into a small crevice and upon making his way back to `Base' shared his find with the others. The twins had immediately relieved him of his prize and he was now getting his first proper look.

`Urgh! That's disgusting. People don't really do that.' Chris said, pointing to a particularly graphic photograph.

`Course they do. Your Mam an' Dad's done it at least four times.' Lee said. `Or do yer still believe yer old man dug you an' yer sisters up from under a gooseberry bush?'

`Well no... but... I just can't see mi Mam letting mi Dad do owt like that.'

`Fuck me, you've got a lot to learn your young uns. She probably enjoys it as much as he does. Look at all them birds in there, they're fuckin loving it!'

`Well I don't want to see any more.' Chris said, putting the magazine down.

`What about you young Westy? What do yer reckon?'

`Well... I walked in on our Nicola an' mi cousin once by accident when they were getting ready for bed an' they were both undressed.'

`Yeah. And?'

`Well... they both had hair... down there an' tits an' that.'

`But?'

`But their fannies dint look owt like that.'

`I told yer, yer've got a lot to learn. Your Nicola's only seventeen her fanny won't get split like that till she's eighteen an' a proper woman. Any road, give us them books back, we'll hide em again an' come back tomorrow for a proper look.'

****

By eight-thirty the next morning Simon had the house to himself. His father and his sister had long since left for their respective jobs and his mother had taken his younger brother to school in Denaby. Simon himself had just finished his first year at Pope Pius X secondary school in Wath. His school came under the control of Rotherham Borough and as a result his school holidays were sometimes slightly different to those of Doncaster, he had `broken up' for the summer on Friday, whereas the schools in the Doncaster catchment area didn't finish until the following Wednesday. This had left him with three days where he had to make his own entertainment, as all his friends out of school went to Northcliffe school here in Conisborough. Today however, he knew exactly how he was going to fill those first few hours of solitude. His mother had her needlework class this morning and so wouldn't be home until at least ten-thirty. That gave him two hours or more to make the short journey from the Bradley Estate where he lived to the Elephant Rock on Minneymoor and have a good look at those mucky books he'd found yesterday. He could be back home awaiting his mothers' return and she need never know he'd been out.

Simon retrieved the illicit material from its hiding place and eagerly prepared to start reading. Just at that moment he heard voices close by. Peering out from his hiding place behind the large rock he saw a middle-aged couple, out walking their dog. He quickly ducked back into cover, breathing heavily. Think I might be a bit too close to the path here, he thought, I'll go further back in the trees. Maybe I'll go to the Cave Rock, no perhaps not, sometimes folk walked their dogs through there as well. I'll go over to Table Rock, that way I'll be able to see anybody coming an' ave time to hide the mags, yeah that's what I'll do. His decision made, Simon rolled up the magazines and tucked them into the waistband of his shorts, before covering them with his t-shirt and setting out across the field. He had only covered half the distance when he changed his mind again. Of course, he thought, The Kings Seat that's the perfect place. To the best of Simons' knowledge none of the adults in the area, and only a few of the children for that matter, ever frequented that particular part of the field. In fact, although a lot of the kids knew the rock was there only a select few were aware of its name. Access to The Kings Seat was gained by means of a short, easy climb to the rocks summit. Here, the natural erosion of the limestone had formed an indentation which, when one sat in it, provided a rough backrest and two armrests. It was here that Simon now sat, perusing the glossy pictures and reading the unbelievable `Readers Stories', sometimes laughing out loud at the images on the pages before him. He had absolutely no idea what purpose a `vibrating penis' could possibly serve, in fact it sounded quite uncomfortable, but for three pounds plus postage and packaging apparently, a man could make his vibrate. On the other hand, they were quite educational these magazines. He'd sometimes heard the older boys at school talking about `lesbians' but never knew what one was but now, thanks to his mornings' reading material, he could rest assured in the knowledge that a lesbian was a young woman with either pink or orange hair who took all her clothes off and pretended to kiss another woman on the arse in a magazine.

It was at this point that Simon checked his watch and was surprised to see that it was almost quarter past ten. He'd better get going, his mother would be home soon. He quickly secreted the magazines in the crevice alongside his seat, he'd tell Carl and Lee later that he'd moved them to a safer hiding place, they'd be well pleased with him. Simon descended from his vantage point and stood at the base of the rock brushing himself down.

Just as he was turning to go he felt himself grabbed roughly from behind. His t-shirt was pulled over his head and he was pushed violently into the face of the rock. He felt his nose explode and became instantly dizzy and nauseous.

`I'm gonna make you squeal yer little bastard!' a voice hissed menacingly in his ear.

Mercifully, Simon was to feel very little of what was done to him for the next hour.

Chapter 2

Tuesday 20th July 1982

3.30 p.m. Hill Top Hotel, Conisborough.

`What's this?' Detective Constable Eric Dalton asked, suspiciously eying the package that had just been dropped into his lap.

`That mi old cock, is me covering mi arse. Call it mi own personal insurance policy if yer like.' Pat O'Hanlon replied.

The two men were sitting in Daltons car, which was parked in the corner of the car park furthest from both the main road and the pub itself. Pat had been the last of the pubs patrons to leave that afternoon. By prior arrangement this coincided with Daltons arrival and now the two men had the car park to themselves in which to conduct their business.

`I don't understand, what do you mean insurance policy?'

`Well, mebbe thy ought to open it an' see. No? Alright then, I'll explain it to yer. What yer've got there is a collection of photos, a written statement giving names, dates an' places, an' a tape recording o' me an' thee discussing some of our little business transactions.'

`But surely this material incriminates you just as much as it does me.' Dalton said as he ripped open the package. `I mean, look, you're in as many photographs as I am.'

`Aye, tha reyt an' that tape recording drops me in as much shit as you an' all.'

`So what's the point? Why now after all this time?'

`Because Eric lad, I've had enough, I'm finished wi it all, done, dusted, I want out. A few joints o' cannabis or Mary Joanna or whatever it's called this week is one thing but that other shit you an' yer mate want to start flogging, I'll ave fuck all to do wi, understand?'

`You can't just walk away not n...'

`I can lad an' I am. I've got half a dozen copies o' that little lot in safe keeping wi half a dozen different folk, folk as you an' yer mate know nowt about. If owt untoward were to happen to me they're all under strict instructions to make the lot public. That includes me getting charged wi any sort o' crime, just in case yer were to try setting me up wi owt. It also covers mi family, so yer can forget going after our Jud or that lad of his to try an' get at me.'

`And how can I be sure that you won't just release all this information at some time in the future anyway?'

`I don't suppose yer can really. Yer'll just ave to take my word for it is all. Look Eric lad, I don't give a fuck if you an' yer mate want to carry on doing what yer doing I just don't want any more part of it an' if you've any sense, yer'll knock it on head yerself.'

`Well it seems my hands are tied. You do know this could be construed as blackmail?

`What yer gonna do, arrest me? No, it's not blackmail son, I've told yer, it's just an insurance. Now t...'

`Hey... just a minute, what's this?' Dalton said, holding up a smaller package that had fallen unnoticed, until now, from the original parcel.

`Ah... now *that* could possibly be construed as blackmail. That old cock is just a little extra incentive, in case yer need one, to leave me be. It's something as is very close to both our hearts, if yer catch mi drift?'

`No... surely... you swore never to tell another soul. You can't do this. Think of the heartache it would cause. You *swore* you'd never tell.'

`Aye, that I did lad an' I've always been a man o' mi word, so just as long as yer do as I've asked an' leave me be, nobody'll hear it from me. Now, don't take this the wrong way young Eric but I hope I never ave cause to speak to thee again.'

The car shook as Pat got out and slammed the door, before making his way over to his old, battered Volvo.

`Shit! Shit! Shit!' cursed Dalton loudly, slamming both hands violently against the steering wheel. A right fucking mess I'm in now, he thought, as he watched Pats' car pull slowly out onto the main road and accelerate away.

Chapter 3

Thursday 22nd July 1982.

10.00 a.m. Windmill Avenue, Conisborough.

`You've been at mi fags again yer little bastard ant yer, where are they?' Graham Blake snarled menacingly at his step-son.

`No I ant, honest. I only smoke Bensons.' Whined nineteen years old Brian Sutton.

`Don't give me that yer little shit, you'd smoke rolled dog shit as long as yer dint have to pay for it. There was a twenty pack wi just one missing on mantelpiece when I went to bed last night an' as yer can see they're not there now.'

`That don't mean I took em, maybe mi Mam took em to work wi her this morning.'

`Don't blame yer Mother, she wouldn't fuckin dare take owt as dint belong to her, she knows what she'd get. Not like you yer thieving, bone-idle, little twat.'

`Look who's talking. You'd know all about bone-idle, sending mi Mam out to work every day an' then taking all her money so's yer can spend all day wi yer mates in Eagle an' bookies. Don't know what she ever saw in you, yer fat, lazy, bastard.'

`You, mouthy little fucker!' Graham lashed out. Once, twice, three times, all vicious, full-blooded punches that caused Brian to fall back onto the settee, covering his head with his arms as his step-father continued to rain blows down on him.

`You ungrateful, little shit! I take you on as if yer were mi own, give yer a fuckin roof over yer head an' you dare to talk to me like that. I always knew yer were no good but yer've gone too far this time. That Mother o' yours is far too soft on yer, well that stops now. Do you hear me?' Graham shouted, stepping back from the settee breathing heavily.

Slowly, Brian uncurled himself and got shakily to his feet, wincing in pain as he did so.

`I think yer've broke mi ribs.' He mumbled.

`Just be grateful I dint break yer fuckin neck. Now, I'm gonna check your bedroom an' if I find mi fags yer'd better make sure yer not here when I get back.'

Graham turned to leave and that's when Brian seized his chance. Ignoring the pain from his ribs he grabbed the poker from its place by the fire. The first blow caught Graham squarely across the shoulders. The second, as he turned back to face his assailant, hit him full in the face and brought him to his knees. Blows three and four, to the top and back of his head, rendered him unconscious.

Brian dropped the poker and stared at the prone figure on the floor in front of him, blood already running freely and mixing with the deep pile of the carpet.

`Yer deserved that yer bastard. I hope I've killed yer.' He said smiling.

Calmly he knelt down and removed the wallet from the rear pocket of his step-fathers' jeans. A five pound note and three ones. It'll do for now he thought, standing back up and making his way painfully upstairs to the bathroom.

An hour later, after a leisurely bath and a change of clothes, he was once more staring down at the figure on the living room floor. He didn't appear to have moved and as far as Brian could tell wasn't breathing. Maybe I *have* killed him, he thought, oh well not to worry. Shrugging his shoulders, he walked out to the kitchen and made himself tea and toast. After finishing his meal, he went to the coat stand in the hallway. Reaching into the pocket of his Mothers' best jacket, he retrieved the packet of cigarettes he had secreted there after his step-father had gone to bed last night. Smiling to himself he lit-up and inhaled deeply, savouring the sudden nicotine rush for a moment, before returning to the kitchen and sitting at the table. Half an hour and three cigarettes later Brian once more returned to the living room. Still no movement from the figure on the floor. He squatted down on his haunches and peered closely at the face before him. Grahams' eyes had rolled back into his head and his skin had taken on a grey pallor. Well yer certainly look dead to me, he thought. Better safe than sorry though. Another trip to the kitchen. This time, when he returned, he was carrying the biggest, sharpest knife he could find. Carefully positioning it above where he believed the heart to be, he pushed down with all his weight. After an initial resistance, he felt the blade ease its way into the body right up to the hilt. He was surprised at how little blood this produced and his step-father didn't move at all. Yer must've been dead after all then. Well there's no point hanging about here.

`Mi Mam's gonna kill you when she sees mess yer've made of her carpet Fat Boy.' He said laughing. `All over a packet o' poxy fags an' all. Yer should've taken notice o' warnings, `Smoking can seriously damage your health.'

Without a backward glance, Brian walked calmly out of the room, down the hallway, and out of the front door, closing it gently and locking it, whistling quietly to himself as he did.

Brian `Pongo' Sutton walked past the Windmill Youth Centre and across the park onto Highfield Road. At the off licence at the bottom of the road he purchased four cans of lager and a couple of packets of crisps then made the short journey along the main road to the top of Minneymoor Field, eventually sitting down at what the local kids called Table Rock and opening a can.

Pongo. He'd gained that nickname during his last couple of years at school. Because of his long, pointed nose and usually scruffy appearance he bore an uncanny resemblance to the character Pongo Snodgrass from the kids' comic Krazy. Mostly he didn't let it bother him but when the younger kids called it him he hated it. However, he had never been much of a fighter and he had learned to try and ignore it.

Brian had never been particularly popular at school, always being regarded as one of the `Duggies' or `Thick' kids. It wasn't his fault that written words never made any sense to him or that numbers frightened him, he didn't think it was anyway. The one subject he did excel at though was geography, he could name the capital city of any country in the world or instantly find any country on a globe or map. His inability to transfer his knowledge onto paper however had put paid to any hope of passing an exam and so he had left school in nineteen-seventy-nine with no qualifications and little hope of gainful employment. His Father had been killed in a mining accident when Brian was just three years old, so his Mother had vetoed any ambitions he might have held to go `darn pit'. This suited Brian, the very thought of going underground terrified him. So, since leaving school Brian had become one of Britain's army of unemployed, living on government hand-outs and petty theft.

Crushing the now empty first can, Brian popped the top on a second, lit a cigarette and lay back, enjoying the contrasting sensations of the cool rock and the warm sun on his exposed arms and legs. A few moments later he awoke with a start, the can of lager slipping from his fingers and rolling off the edge of the rock.

`Shit!

He clambered down from his position and bent to retrieve the can that was now spewing its frothy contents onto the grass at the rocks base. It was then that he noticed something tucked into a hollow in the ground almost hidden by a clump of nettles. Brian trampled the nettles down and then carefully reached into the hollow to remove the object. A pair of boys' underpants, a t-shirt, and a pair of shorts had been rolled together, all had traces of what could only be blood on them. He climbed back onto the rock, lit another cigarette and smoked while he thought about his discovery. The t-shirt was one of those transfer jobs that you could get done on Doncaster market. This one depicted the album cover of AC/DC's `Highway to Hell'. Brian knew where he had seen this shirt recently. That young lad off o' Bradley Estate that disappeared a couple o' days back had one just like it, he'd been wearing it a couple of weeks back on this very field when him an' his mates had been taunting Brian and then running off.

`Pongo, Pongo you're so slow. Two add two, you don't know.'

Thinking about this now a smile slowly appeared on Brian's face.

`The coppers won't find yer wi'out clues yer gobby little bastard.' He said out loud.

He then spent a few minutes gathering some dried grass and twigs from his surroundings which he placed in a pile in the centre of the rock before applying the flame from his lighter.

Ten minutes later the last traces of young Simon West were little more than charred and melted rags.

Brian `Pongo' Sutton opened another can of lager, lit another cigarette and lay back smiling. Today had been one of the best days of his whole life he thought happily.

Chapter 4

Thursday 29th July 1982.

CID Headquarters, Doncaster.

I'm too bloody old for this, thought Detective Chief Inspector Cedric Short. Why now? Three sodding weeks till I retire and not one, but *two* major investigations flare up at the same time. Barely a week later and both seem to have ground to a halt and be heading nowhere. Sighing he reached into the pocket of his jacket, which hung on the back of his chair, and removed a battered, brown leather pouch. From the rack on his desk he selected what he always thought of as his `Thinking Pipe'. This was a long briar pipe which he smoked in deference to his literary hero Sherlock Holmes. Contrary to the popular image which depicted Holmes wearing a deerstalker hat and smoking a calabash pipe, Cedric was enough of a Conan Doyle aficionado to know that both were inventions for stage and screen, the curved calabash being adopted in an attempt to avoid hiding the actors face, and that the Sherlock Holmes of the literary world smoked either briar, clay, or Cherrywood pipes. Cedric had one of each, but the briar was his particular favourite and he liked to think that his hero also turned to the same when mulling over one of his `three pipe problems'. He filled the pipes bowl with tobacco from his pouch and lit up using a wooden match. When he had his smoke going satisfactorily, he leaned back in his chair and propped his feet up on the desk, the aromatic smoke quickly filling the small room, as he allowed his mind to wander.

Almost thirty-seven years he'd been a copper, he thought now, having joined the force shortly after the end of the war. Twenty-eight he'd been then, married with two sons, one of whom he had met for the first time upon his return from foreign shores. Like Doctor Watson he too carried a war wound, Nazi shrapnel from El Alamein rather than a

Jezail bullet from Afghanistan but still, he rather liked the comparison. Before hostilities commenced he had been training to be a veterinary surgeon but after the war he had foregone his studies and joined the police force. A number of promotions had followed over the years but fifteen years ago upon reaching his present position of D.C.I. he had also reached the limits of his ambitions. Any further up the ladder, in his opinion, would expose him to far too much of the red tape and bureaucracy that he abhorred and prevent him from doing what he always called `proper coppering'. Luckily Naomi, his long-suffering wife of forty-five years, possessed even less ambition and had absolutely no desire for what she termed `the social climbing of the police royalty'. Happy to have her husband home in time for dinner, most evenings at least, being the wife of a D.C.I. was, if not exactly ideal, certainly bearable and allowed her to shun most of the limelight that the wives of some of the other more senior officers seemed to crave so badly. Three more weeks and they'd both be out of it. The appeal of that little cottage in the Cotswolds grew stronger with every passing day. I might even take up beekeeping like all the best detectives do when they retire, he smiled to himself. Nay, sod that, long walks and even longer pub lunches, the occasional round of golf, which they both enjoyed, that's what they had planned for their twilight years. However, he had no intention of riding off into the sunset and leaving a trail of unsolved cases behind him, he thought now as he refilled and relit his pipe. This murder in Conisborough shouldn't take long to clear up. It seemed pretty obvious that the step-son had finally cracked after years of abuse at the hands of his mothers' spouse. Finding the little bastard was proving to be more difficult than first anticipated though. How the hell a kid with the mental capacity his mother described had managed to elude them for a whole week was verging on the point of embarrassing. Still, Cedric felt sure that he'd turn up sooner rather than later. No, it was the other case that really bothered him. An eleven-year old boy is seen by a neighbour locking his front door shortly after eight-thirty on a Tuesday morning and then nothing, he just disappears. Over the years Cedric had investigated more than his fair share of missing persons' cases and many of them had never been solved. Sometimes, if somebody wanted to disappear badly enough there was nothing could be done to find them. This one however just felt wrong on so many levels. Call it a coppers nose, gut instinct, or whatever else but Cedric held out very little hope of ever finding Simon West alive and was already subconsciously treating the investigation like a murder inquiry. A murder investigation with no body, no suspects, nothing. Unlike the Sutton boy in the other case, Simon it seemed came from a very happy home, got on well with both of his parents, and was a popular boy both at school and at home. He even got on with his older-sister for Christs' sake, which for a kid of that age was a first in Cedrics' experience.

He checked his watch now, five-fifteen as near as damn it. Bugger it, he thought, I'll smoke mesen another pipe an' if nowt else comes up I'll get off home, I'm sure she said it were toad-in-hole tonight an' nobody does toads better than that woman o' mine, he smiled.

Ten minutes later he was shrugging into his jacket when there was a knock on the door.

`Come.'

`Thought you'd like to know straight away Sir...' Detective Sergeant Bill Quinn said as he walked in. `We've found Brian Sutton.'

`Really? Where?'

`Believe it or not he's been living rough but decided to go back to his Mams for a bath an' a change o' clothes. A neighbour saw him unlocking front door an' phoned it in.'

`Where is he now?'

`They're bringing him straight here Sir. Allowing for traffic, I reckon twenty minutes or so.'

`Okay, thanks Bill, I'll be with you shortly.'

When Quinn had gone Cedric picked up his desk phone and dialled a number. A few moments later he heard his wifes voice.

`Naomi? It's only me love. Look I'm sorry but it looks like being a late one, God alone knows what time I'm going to get away.' He paused and listened for a few moments.

`Yes love I know it's my favourite but this really can't wait...' another pause. `Well that's just bloody marvellous... no I know it's not your fault... right yes I'll call when I'm on my way, bye now.'

Cedric slammed down the phone angrily.

`Right you little bastard, missing toad-in-hole's one thing but home-made rhubarb an' apple crumble for afters is taking the piss!' He said to the empty office before storming out, slamming the door behind him.

Chapter 5

8.15 p.m.

Interview Room 1, CID Headquarters, Doncaster.

Cedric Short sat back in his chair and relit his pipe, the Cherrywood this time as he felt it gave him a more professional appearance than his preferred briar, and eyed the youth sitting across the table from him. Throughout his lengthy career, Cedric had found that young offenders usually fell into one of two categories. There was the arrogant, sullen, `no comment', wannabe hard man or the petrified, `I'll tell you anything you want to know, I just want to go home' individual. Brian Sutton however fitted neither of these profiles. Instead, he appeared to be extremely comfortable, content even, with the surroundings in which he now found himself and against all advice to the contrary from the duty solicitor was answering all the questions asked of him with a surprising candour.

`So let's just run through that again Brian.' Bill Quinn was saying now. `Your step-father accused you of stealing cigarettes from him and when you denied it he proceeded to beat you?'

`Started to kick the living shit out o' me is what the fat bastard did more like.'

`Whatever. But at some point, you managed to break free, grab the poker and hit him with it. Am I right so far?'

`I dint break free, he'd stopped hitting me an' said he were gonna search mi bedroom an' if he found the fags I were gonna get some more. He turned his back an' that's when I grabbed the poker an' let him have it.'

`How many times did you hit him Brian?'

`Four... I think. I know the second one were a beauty, caught him full in face it did.' Brian said with a satisfied grin.

`And then you went and had a bath?'

`Yeah, that's right.'

`What just like that?' Cedric asked now. `You've just murdered your step-dad and the first thing you can think of is a nice soak in the bath?'

`I weren't sure as he were dead then.' Brian said. `An' any road mi ribs were killing me an' mi Mam always says a good hot bath's the thing for aching bones.'

`And she'd be right young Brian but that's not what I meant. I mean, didn't you check for a pulse? Were you not afraid that someone might come and discover what you'd done? Didn't you think to maybe call for help before going upstairs and running a bath for yourself?'

`I dint want the bastard to have any help did I? What'd be point in cracking him wi poker an' then trying to help the fucker? An' like I said, mi ribs were killing.'

`Okay, we'll come back to that in a bit. So, you had a nice long soak, got dressed and...?'

`I made mesen a pot o' tea an' some toast then had a smoke.'

`So, you sat in the kitchen drinking tea and smoking while just a few feet away your step-father lay dead or dying on the living room floor?'

`Yeah. They were his fags an' all.' Laughed Brian. `I'd nicked em when the fat twat went to bed an' hid em in mi Mams coat.'

`So, what happened next Brian?'

`Well, after a bit, I went in an' checked on him. His eyes looked all weird an' his face ad gone a reyt funny colour. That's when I thought as I'd maybe killed him for real.'

`So then you decided you'd stab him just to make sure?' asked Quinn.

`Yeah. I dint want the bastard waking up an' coming looking for me, or worse trying to get mi Mam on his side when she got in. So, I got the big knife out o' kitchen an' stuck it in him. He never made a move, so he must o' bin dead all along.'

`I see. And then?'

`I went down to shop an' got mesen a few cans an' some crisps an' had mesen a little drink to celebrate.'

`Forgive me Brian but you don't seem particularly bothered by any of your actions.' Cedric said.

`Cos I'm not. Killing that bastard is the best thing I've ever done in mi life. I did both me an' mi Mam a favour. It were good riddance to bad rubbish, not like that young un as I killed a few days afore. He'd probly never done owt w...'

`Whoah! Hold it right there young man. What the hell do you mean?'

`That kid as disappeared off o' Bradley Estate other week, that were me. You'll never find him though.'

`Let me get this straight. Are you admitting to the murder of Simon West?'

`Aye, that's right. I dint just kill him though, I gave him a right good fuckin before.' Brian said laughing.

Chapter 6

`You little bastard! I'll fuckin kill yer!' Quinn lunged across the table and grabbed hold of Brian's shirt roughly.

`That's enough Sergeant! Let him go... That's an order Quinn.' Cedric said, putting a restraining arm across Quinn's chest.

Reluctantly Quinn released his grip on the young man and sat back down.

`Right, that's better.' Cedric said pleasantly. ` I think this may be an appropriate time to take a break and allow you some time alone with your client Mr. Doyle.'

`Couldn't agree more Chief Inspector and perhaps the raging bull there might take the opportunity to calm himself down a touch.' The duty solicitor said with a raised eyebrow.

`Quite. Interview suspended twenty thirty-seven hours. Sergeant Quinn, with me if you please.'

****

`Right, do you mind telling me just what the *fuckin* hell you were playing at in there Bill?' Cedric said angrily a few moments later. `You're supposed to be an experienced police officer for fucks sake!'

The two detectives were back in Shorts office having called off at the vending machine for two cups of what had to pass for coffee at this time of night.

I've fuckin done it this time, thought Quinn, `The Old Man' never used the f-word and now he'd received two fucks in the same bollocking.

`I'm sorry Sir. Mi temper just got the better of me. When he said as he'd done for the West lad I just saw red, I've got a boy about the same age an' when he started laughing about what he'd done I couldn't help it.'

`No excuse Bill. I've got grandkids that age but when you do this job that's the sort of shit you have to deal with, almost on a daily basis. I shouldn't have to tell you that. It's not as if you're some still wet behind the ears P.C. If you can't conduct yourself in a more professional manner, then now's the time to tell me.'

`It won't happen again sir, I promise.'

`It better not, I won't tolerate that sort of behaviour from anyone on my team, whatever the provocation. Listen son, you're what thirty-three? Thirty-four?'

`Thirty-five next week Sir.'

`Thirty-five, you've probably got another thirty years of the job in front of you. You're a bloody good copper Bill and there's no reason why you can't go right to the top, just so long as you learn to control yourself. Take a bit of advice lad, when you put your jacket on and leave home you're Detective Sergeant William Quinn and whatever you left behind you when you closed that front door stays there until such time as you return and take your jacket off again. That's when you can go back to being good old Bill to your lass, no pun intended, and Dad or Daddy to the kids. Learn to separate the two lad, else this job will be the death of you. Now, do you think you've calmed down sufficiently to continue the interview without us risking an accusation of police brutality?'

`Yes Sir, of course Sir.'

`Excellent. Let's get a move-on then. I'd like to get to my crumble afore midnight, plays hell with mi digestive system otherwise.'

Chapter 7

Friday 30th July 1982

CID Headquarters, Doncaster.

`Ah Cedric, close the door and take a seat.' Chief Constable Edward Baker smiled from behind his desk.

`Thankyou Sir.' Short said taking the chair opposite.

`Drink?' Baker asked.

`Er... no thanks s...'

`Nonsense.' Baker said good-naturedly. `It's not every day we find ourselves with so much to celebrate.' Baker poured two generous measures of brandy into cut-glass tumblers from the matching decanter on his desk and handed one to Cedric. `Cheers.'

`Cheers Sir.'

Both men took a sip from their drinks and then Baker unwrapped a cigar.

`Fill yourself a pipe Cedric, a man should always enjoy a smoke whilst partaking in a fine brandy in my opinion.'

`Thankyou Sir.'

The two men sat in contented silence for a few minutes, each enjoying the warming sensation of the brandy combined with the calming effect of their respective smokes.

`I must say, that was excellent work last evening Cedric, really top-drawer. Two cases put to bed within a matter of hours. What a way to bring the curtain down on a glittering career eh?'

`Thankyou Sir but I'm not altogether sure we can close the Simon West inquiry just at the m...'

`Why ever not man? We've got a confession for Christs sake.'

`Something just doesn't feel right. Oh, I've no doubt the Sutton lad's responsible for killing his step-father but I just don't see him as a child-killer.'

`Then why the hell would he confess? The boy's a killer, if he can do for a man bigger and stronger than himself then I can't see him having any problem with a mere child.'

`He'd good reason for killing Graham Blake, the man was a wife-beater and abusive father. Truth be known he's no great loss but it's still against the law so Sutton will pay the price for his crime. No, my point is that was done in the heat of the moment, the West boy's a different kettle of fish altogether. I mean we don't even know for sure that the poor sod's dead. He might just have run away from home.'

`Oh come off it Cedric, it's only the other day that you said, right in this very office I might add, that you didn't hold out much hope of ever finding him alive. Now you've got a signed confession to his murder and you want to continue with a missing persons inquiry. What the bloody hell's your problem?'

`It's my gut feeling is all Sir. I think there's more to this than meets the eye.'

`You and your bloody gut feelings! Have you any idea how many times they've held you back during your career? If you'd not been so bloody pig-headed over the years you could have been sitting in this chair, or in one even further up the chain. Instead you've spent the last fifteen years stuck in the role of DCI chasing your arse with your bloody `proper coppering' ideals.'

`My `bloody gut feelings' have also given me a success rate in all major inquiries that's second to none Sir.'

`And now you want to piss it all away because you've got a confession that doesn't *feel* right.'

`In all my years on the job Sir I've never knowingly sent down an innocent man, I don't want to start now.'

`Oh for Christs sake, he's not bloody innocent, he's confessed. He's even described what the boy was wearing man. How could he know that if he weren't guilty eh? As far as I'm aware his own mother couldn't be a hundred per-cent sure at the time but she's confirmed that her son owned articles of clothing such as Sutton described.'

`He could have seen the boy dressed like that on any number of occasions Sir. After all, they lived less than a mile from one another.'

`Bollocks Cedric. No, I'm sorry, as far as I'm concerned we've got enough evidence to charge Brian Sutton with the murders of both Graham Blake *and* Simon West, regardless of whether or not we find the poor sods body and that's an end to it.'

`For the record Sir, I think you're making a big mistake.'

`Don't let that worry you too much old friend. In three weeks' time you'll be done with all this and four months after that I shall follow you into the ranks of the happily retired. Let it go Cedric, enjoy the golf or the fishing, or whatever you've got planned, knowing you can look back with pride on a long and illustrious career. That'd be my advice anyway.'

`Whatever you say Sir. I just hope this doesn't come back to bite us all on our arses that's all.'

`I think you'll find that I have my arse sufficiently covered.' Baker laughed.

Now why does that not surprise me thought Cedric as he rose from his chair and with a nod to his superior left the office.

Chapter 8

Saturday 21st August 1982, 9.30 p.m.

Town Moor Golf Club, Doncaster.

Cedric Short tamped the tobacco down into the bowl of his pipe, applied a light from a wooden match and puffed away until he was satisfied with the results. Perched on the end of a table in the patioed area of the club he looked out over the eighteenth green. How many times over the years, he wondered, had he walked up the fairway towards that immaculately manicured patch of green. Hundreds? Thousands? Would he ever walk these hallowed grounds again? Over the years he'd been lucky enough to play on some of the best courses in the land and more than just a few in other lands as well. So what was it about this course that he held so dear? Could it really compare to The Belfry or St. Andrews? No, not in a million years. It's because it was home he realised now. He'd been a member here long before it became a full eighteen-hole course in nineteen-sixty-five and in all that time, work commitments and holidays permitting, he had played at least once, sometimes as often as three times a week. He and Naomi had already applied for membership at a course close to their retirement cottage in The Cotswolds but somehow, he doubted it would live up to this old girl. He resolved there and then that he was going to make the effort to return and play here at least a couple of weekends each year.

`Penny for em Sir?'

Startled, Cedric turned sharply.

`Oh it's you Bill. What brings you out here?'

`I was just getting a refill at the bar when I happened to glance out the window an' see yer puffing away at that old pipe o' yours. So, I thought to mesen `why's the boss standing out there all on his own while everybody else is inside getting pissed up at his party' then I thought yer might like one o' these.' Quinn passed over a generous measure of amber coloured liquid. `Single-malt Sir, just as yer like.'

`And how would you know my favourite tipple Bill? As far as I can recall, any time you and I have had cause to call for a drink together, strictly in the line of duty of course, we've never had more than two or three pints at most. You're quite partial to a drop of Tetley if memory serves me right.'

`That's right Sir. But it might surprise you to know that you're not the only detective here tonight. I snuck a peek in your desk drawer one day last week an' checked the label on the bottle you keep in there an' just to be on the safe side, I took the liberty of asking Mrs. Short to confirm it just before I came out here.' Quinn smiled as he lit a cigarette.

`Well bugger me.' Laughed Cedric. `Yer might make the bloody grade yet lad.'

`I'd just like to take the chance to wish yer all the best for your retirement Sir. I'm sure the whole team's gonna miss yer, the place won't be same wi'out yer.'

`Don't be getting all sentimental on me now lad but I thank yer all the same. I meant what I said the other week an' all lad, yer a bloody good copper an' you've got the potential to go a long way.'

`Thankyou Sir. Do you mind if I ask you a question?'

`Go on lad.'

`Is there any reason you never went further than DCI? I mean, there can't be a copper in land as knows the job better than you.'

`A lack of ambition coupled with an inability to do as I'm told Bill. Suppose I ought to be grateful I made it as far as I did if I'm honest.'

`In that case Sir, if yer don't mind me saying, what makes yer think I'll do any better, especially now you won't be there to keep me on the straight an' narrow.'

Bill Quinn winked at his erstwhile boss and started to make his way back inside.

`Bill?'

`Yes Sir?'

`Oh never mind, it doesn't matter. I'll see you inside in a minute.

****

Later that evening as he and Naomi were making their way upstairs Cedric noticed a package on the hall table.

`What's this love?'

`I don't know, I didn't open it. It came this afternoon and I forgot all about it.'

Carefully he unwrapped the package. Inside was a display case containing three bottles of single-malt scotch. Underneath the scotch was a leather-bound book. Cedric examined this carefully.

`The Complete Sherlock Holmes Stories' by `Sir Arthur Conan Doyle'.

He opened the inside cover to where someone had written a dedication.

`TO THE GREATEST DETECTIVE OF THEM ALL' THANKS, BILL.

`Well the dozy little sod. This little lot must've cost him a month's wages.' He said, wiping a tear from his eye.

PART TWO

PRESENT DAY

Chapter 9

Sunday 8th January 2017, 2.00.p.m.

Hill Top Hotel, Conisborough.

`An' get one for yer self Beth lass.' Jud O'Hanlon said passing a note over to the young girl behind the bar.

`No thanks I'm fine Jud, still a bit hungover from last night to be honest.'

`Go anywhere nice did yer lass?'

`Just to town wi a couple o' mi mates but we dint get in till about three o'clock an' I had to be here to start work at half eleven.' Beth said, handing over a few coins in change.

`You younguns, does tha know when I were your age I used to be out on piss Friday night, Saturday afternoon an' night, Sunday afternoon, Sunday night an' still be up at four o'clock Monday morning to walk to pit for mi shift.'

`An' you did all that when you were my age Jud? You must ave a good memory t... oh shit.' She said looking over Juds shoulder.

Puzzled, Jud turned around to see a young man making his way from the tap room door to the bar. Twenty-five, possibly twenty-six, a shade over six feet tall. He walked with that pathetic swagger that the young lads today all seemed to think gave them an air of menace. To Jud they just looked as though they must've had a bad case of polio as children.

`Well if it int the little cock teaser.' The youth sneered as he approached the bar.

`Just leave me alone will yer? I told yer last night, I'm not interested.' Beth said.

`Yer were fuckin interested enough last night when yer were drinking jaeger bombs that I paid for though, weren't yer?'

`Yer bought me one drink an' that's only cos they were two for one an' I dint want it anyway. I only took it cos I felt sorry for yer cos yer mates had pissed off an' left yer. I can see why now.' Beth said looking at the lad disgustedly.

`Yer fuckin slag…'

`Now then, there's no need for that lad.'

`Fuck off Grandad, this is nowt to do wi you.'

`Be very careful son.' Jud said menacingly.

`Just keep out of it yer silly old cunt. I'm talking to this bitch n…'

The young man never got the chance to finish his sentence. George O'Hanlon stood at six feet three inches tall and weighed more than seventeen stones. Although only a month short of his seventieth birthday there was very little fat on his bulky frame. For a man of his size he also possessed a remarkable turn of speed. In one swift movement, he grabbed the youth by the hair and slammed him face-first into the top of the bar before dragging him upright once more.

`Now then yer little gob shite, apologise to the young lassie.' He said calmly.

`I'm sorry.' Mumbled the youth almost inaudibly.

`Did yer get that Beth?'

Staring wide-eyed at the young mans bloodied face, she just nodded mutely.

`Right then off we go.'

At this, Jud swiftly frog-marched the youth out into the car-park.

`Which is your motor? Come on, I ant got all bastard day.'

The lad nodded towards a red Mazda.

`Reyt then. Open it.'

`It's unlocked.' He mumbled.

`Now you listen to me an' yer listen good cos I'm not in habit o' repeating mesen. I don't ever want to see your ugly fuckin face round here again ave yer got me? Yer keep well away from that lass in there at all times. Even if yer see her in town yer look the other way, understand?'

The youth nodded.

`I said, do yer understand?'

`Y...yeah.'

`I'm not sure as yer do.'

Jud grabbed the young man by the right wrist and forced his hand into the cars door jamb before viciously slamming the door and leaning his considerable weight against it. The lads screams reminded Jud of the time he'd helped Grandad Danny slaughter a pig in the backyard sixty-odd years before.

`Now then lad, I reckon as I've probably just broken most o' bones in that hand o' thine an' guess what? I don't give a fuck, that's just me playing nice. I meant what I said lad, yer do as I've told yer or next time I might get nasty. Drive careful now won't yer?'

A few moments later Jud walked back into the tap room to a round of applause from the dozen or so customers. Never one to miss an opportunity he bowed to the small crowd.

`Thank you, thank you... you're all so kind.' He smiled, as he made his way to the bar.

`Thank you Jud.' Said Beth smiling.

`No problem darling. Just cos you *are* a bitch that dunt gi' that little bastard the right to say so.' Jud winked. `I'm only kidding love.'

`No yer reyt Jud. It takes a bitch like me to put up wi' a bastard like you.' Beth smiled, winked, and walked into the other side of the bar.

`Well, fuck me drunk.' Jud laughed and, collecting his drinks made his way to the table where his family waited.

****

`Nice to know some things never change Dad. Yer've still got it old man.' Juds son Peter smiled at his father.

`Aw come on now Peter, stop it, will you not encourage the feckin great oaf.' Katie O'Hanlon admonished her son.

`No Mam, fair's fair. Yer've got to admit the auld feller were quite impressive there. He must o' bin giving that young un forty-five years or more an' look at him, he's not even breathing heavy, or breaking sweat either.'

`Well I ought to know better than to expect any different from you. It's your Fathers son you are an' no mistake, cut from the same cloth the two o' ye. Logan, will you not agree with me though? The feckin eejit should know better at his age.'

`Well Katie… he was defending a young girls honour, in a manner of speaking.' Logan Harvey, Jud and Katies son-in-law, said.

`Was he shite! He was playing the feckin big man. The same way he's been doing ever since I first clapped eyes on him, all those years ago.'

`Mam's got a point Dad.' Niamh Harvey said now. `After all yer nearly seventy now.'

`Aye lass an' I've bin sorting out sacks o' shit like that for most o' them seventy years an' all. Don't you worry about yer old man love, I'll be able to handle the likes o' yon when I'm ninety. Mind yer I reckon he'll think twice afore trying me again eh? All that aggro just cos young Beth dint jump into bed wi' him. When a man gets to my age he realises as that nookie game's overrated anyway an' that he'd rather ave an extra Yorkshire wi' his Sunday dinner.' Jud said, to a chorus of laughter from the men at the table.

`Yes and when a woman gets to my age *she* realises that she has more chance of getting a rise out of the feckin puddings anyhow!' Katies comment had the whole table laughing hysterically.

`Yer cheeky…' but even Jud had to join in the laughter.

Sitting almost unnoticed, with the exception of a couple of admiring glances from some of the men present when she'd first walked in, Grace Morgan sipped from her glass of white wine, occasionally glancing across the small tap room at the family opposite.

Yes, she thought, that must be him. He fitted every description she'd been given during her discreet enquiries; age, height, physique, all tallied and if the spectacle she'd just witnessed was anything to go by, a short fuse and a propensity for violence to go with it. This had to be the man she sought, she had found `Big Jud' O'Hanlon.

How to go about engineering a meeting though? She couldn't just walk up to his table and boldly introduce herself, could she? No, not while he was enjoying a `quiet' Sunday afternoon with his family. Maybe she could wait until he came to the bar again and somehow `accidentally' bump into him? Don't be stupid Grace, this isn't some bloke that's caught your eye across the room in some pub in town, you're not chasing some `bit o' rough' just to prove to yourself you've still got it, save that sort of behaviour for Friday nights with the girls. No, this is serious and you'd better start thinking of a way to do what you came to do before you lose your nerve and chicken out. Picking up her glass once more, she drank the remainder of her wine, before standing up and covering the few short steps to the bar.

`Large dry white wine please.' She said to the young woman, who seemed remarkably unperturbed by the events of only half an hour earlier.

`I like your top.' Beth said, handing over her change a few moments later.

`Thank you, I made it myself.'

`Really?'

`Well, I should say I designed it and a friend in London actually made it for me. My name's Grace by the way.'

`I'm Bethany. I've got a niece called Grace, she's only two but she's a right little bugger.'

`We must all be the same.' Laughed Grace.

`Talented as well as beautiful eh? Pint o' bitter, pint o' blonde, an' a pint o' lager please Beth love.'

Beth stifled a giggle as Grace rolled her eyes before turning to face the man who had spoken. Peter O'Hanlon stood grinning at her.

`Not seen you round here before love, just passing through are yer?'

`In a manner of speaking yes. I was brought up just down the road in Clifton but I moved to London years ago. I'm just up for my Mother's funeral.'

`Oh, sorry to hear that.'

`No need, we weren't particularly close.'

`Half a lager an' a vodka an' diet coke please. Want another in there love?'

`No thanks, I'll be fine with this for the moment.'

`Pay her one on.' Pete said handing over a twenty. `Are yer waiting for somebody or do yer always drink alone?'

`I just got fed up staring at four walls and somebody told me the food in here was excellent. I didn't know the kitchen was closed obviously.'

`Aye, John an' Julie, that's the owners, always go away week after New Year. Tell thi what, why don't yer come over an' sit wi' us for a bit. We're gonna ave a few more drinks an' about seven o' clock we're off down the road for a curry. They do a cracking Balti.'

`No, I couldn't possibly intrude.' You stupid bitch, this is the chance you've been waiting for!

`Dunt be daft. Come on, grab yer drink an' bring that vodka an' all. I'll introduce yer to tribe.'

The biggest pair of hands Grace had ever seen then enveloped three pint glasses and the half of lager.

`Come on lass, what yer waiting for?'

****

The next three hours were some of the most enjoyable Grace could ever remember. Far from what she'd expected, from what little she'd been told and the altercation she'd witnessed earlier, Jud proved to be quite the most charming and entertaining of men. His wife, Katie, was a delight, she reminded Grace of a smaller version of televisions Mrs. Brown. Niamh and Logan made a lovely couple and Peter..., well if she could be said to have a `type', then he was certainly it. Under other circumstances who knows what could have happened? All of this now conspired to make her feel every inch the fraud she knew herself to be. However, she'd come this far. Steeling herself, she drained the contents of her glass.

`Yer ready for another there love? It's my shout I think.' Jud said starting to get out of his seat.

`No, not just at the moment. I'm afraid that I haven't been entirely honest with you all.'

`Oh aye? Well yer'd best alter that now then, ant yer lass?' Jud sat back down.

`You see the thing is, I believe that you knew my Father, well, what I mean is I *know* that you knew him. Oh God! I'm not making much sense, am I?'

`None whatsoever but go on lass, spit it out, we'll sort it.' Jud said.

`The man that for forty-five years I have believed to be my Father was Eric Dalton, Detective Chief Inspector Eric Dalton.'

`That fuckin shithouse!'

`George! For the love o' God hold your tongue and let the poor girl finish, can you not see she's upset?' Katie admonished. `Go on sweetheart, you say that you *believed* he was your Father?'

`Yes.' Grace nodded, took a deep breath and continued. `Two days ago I discovered that I am in fact the result of an affair between my Mother and... Patrick O'Hanlon, your uncle I believe Jud?'

There was a stunned silence around the table at this revelation. Peter, who had been in the process of finishing his drink almost choked on the last dregs and began to cough and splutter loudly.

`I'm assuming as yer've got some sort o' evidence to back up what yer saying lass.' Jud said when he'd recovered sufficiently.

`Well I don't have any DNA charts that prove inconclusively that Patrick is my father if that's what you mean.'

`What is it that's led you to this conclusion, if yer don't mind me asking?' Logan said.

`Eric Dalton, as I'm sure you all know was murdered last November.'

`Know about it? Logan here helped to track down the killers, dint yer Loge?'

`That's not strictly true Pete, as you well know, I just helped the police with some historical elements of their investigation.'

`Leave it out wi false modesty Loge. Yer old man were first victim an' that Williams feller refused to confess unless you were there wi him.'

`Again not strictly true but please carry on Grace.'

`Two days after Christmas he was laid to rest with all the pomp and ceremony you might expect. That same night my Mother took an overdose of gin and sleeping tablets, she was found two days later. I won't lie to you, I wasn't close to any of my parents, in actual fact, I didn't even bother making the journey from London for my Dads funeral.'

`Can't say as I blame yer there.' Muttered Jud.

`George! For fecks sake, at least have a *bit* of respect.'

`Yes, my little banshee. Go on lass.'

`We buried Mum on Thursday and I've spent the last couple of days sorting through all of her and Dads things. Right at the back of Mums wardrobe was a large parcel with my name written in large capital letters on it. Inside were a number of documents, photographs, and a letter, again with my name on it. In the letter, amongst other things, Mum admits to her affair with your uncle. She goes on to say that there's no doubt that I'm Patricks daughter because Dad was unable to father children because of a low sperm count...'

`HA, HA, HA.' Jud suddenly burst out laughing. `This is brilliant, Eric `high an' mighty' Dalton were a fuckin Jaffa. Beth, Beth, get us another round o' drinks in, I'll come an' get em in a minute. Aww, this is fuckin magic.' He called over to the bar.

`George! For f...'

`No, it's alright Katie.' Grace said and Katie was shocked to see the younger woman struggling to contain her own laughter.

`Jesus, Mary, and Joseph. Am I the only sane one among us?' She said as she crossed herself.

`My Father wasn't a nice man Katie. In fact, I'd go as far as saying that at times he was a right evil bastard. That doesn't mean to say however that I think he deserved to die the way he did. I'm sorry if it offends you that, like your husband, I'm able to find some amusement in his shortcomings.'

`Shortcomings! Oh Christ, that's a good one lass. Yer do know, don't yer Grace? That makes you what we used to call a grudge baby.'

`I'm not sure I follow Jud.'

`Somebody had it in for yer old man.' Jud was now almost howling with laughter. ` Here Pete, go get them drinks will yer?' Jud passed his son a twenty-pound note. `I'm off to back afore I piss mesen. Shortcomings, Dalton the Dud. Fuck me, I don't think I can take much more o' this.' And off he went to the toilets, shoulders still shaking with mirth as he left.

`Oh that feckin great clown! I swear that one day I'll die from the sheer embarrassment of being married to it and the pair of you can straighten your faces as well, he hardly needs the encouragement.' Katie looked sharply at Logan and Niamh.

****

`Did you bring any of these documents with you?' Logan asked a few minutes later.

They were, all six of them, gathered at the smoke shelter outside. Everybody, even Jud, had managed to regain at least some vestige of composure.

`No, to be honest, I wasn't entirely sure that I'd be able to bring myself to approach you, so I decided to leave them at the house. I'm not due back in London until next Saturday though so I can drop them off any time before then.'

`Just drop em in wi Logan, there's nowt he likes better than looking through old documents an' shite like that.' Pete said.

`I will of course but I must warn you, none of the material paints either Dad or Patrick in a very favourable light. In actual fact, most of it provides evidence that the pair of them were involved in a number of illegal activities during the late seventies and early eighties.'

`So he weren't just a Jaffa, he were a bent Jaffa to boot.'

`George don't start all that nonsense again.' Pleaded Katie.

`No, no I'm not honest but it seems we've found the answer to one family mystery anyway.'

`Which is?' Grace asked.

`I always knew our Pat had summat on yer old man but he never let on what it was.'

`Well, like I said Jud, these papers are evidence of a number of crimes committed by Dad and Pat, or perhaps I should just refer to them as my two Dads.' She added smiling.

`What sort of crimes?' asked Logan.

`The supply of cannabis mainly. It seems, from what little I've read, that Patrick had secretly been keeping records of every transaction and had later used these same records as some kind of leverage with which to extricate himself from any further dealings. Whatever reason he had for wanting out of their arrangement, he used this information to that end.'

`Well, there's nowt as any of us can do about it tonight, so I propose we get back inside, ave a couple more drinks, an' then see about that curry. Any amendments to my proposal... no? right that's carried then. Logan, it's your round lad.'

Chapter 10

Monday 9th January 2017 8.15 a.m.

Minneymoor field, Conisborough.

`Prince! Prince! C'mon boy.'

What's the little twat up to? Thought Dave Chadwick as he watched his border collie go darting through the recently cleared overgrowth near the top corner of the field.

`Prince!' he shouted again now. `C'mon lad.'

This is not like him, he thought, the dog was normally very obedient and came back at the first command. As he drew closer he could see Prince madly scrabbling at the ground, close to the base of a rock which had recently been uncovered during the councils' extensive tidy-up of recent weeks. Now that he was almost upon the dog he could hear Prince making a high-pitched whining sound as he continued frantically pawing the ground.

`What is it boy? C'mon, let's ave a look.'

Gently but firmly he eased the dog away and clipped his lead to the collar.

`Easy lad. What yer found then eh?... `Aww Christ no... sweet, suffering Jesus. Come away lad, c'mon.'

Dave staggered backwards, pulling firmly at the dogs' lead and simultaneously fumbling in his jacket pocket for his phone. A few feet away, at the spot where Prince had just been scratching, the unmistakable form of a human skull protruded from the ground.

Chapter 11

Monday 9th January 2017, 9.15.a.m

Minneymoor Field, Conisborough

`...All I'm saying D.J. is that it's a very popular form of music that has a massive following in this country. I mean, come on man some of those Northern Soul dos are huge events, packed to the rafters in most cases.'

`Aye Troy, I'm not denying any o' that an' each to their own but all *I'm* saying is that a fifty-something bloke spinning records dunt constitute live music. If that were the case, every time yer put a c.d. on at home, or in car, yer might as well call it a concert. No mi old cocker, if yer want live music then yer Classic Rock's the way to go. I don't care how good yer sound system is, if all's yer've got is a record player it int live. A couple o' guitars, a bass, an' a drum kit, an' obviously the ability to play em, then yer've got yerself a concert, ergo *live music*.'

`But some of the biggest names in the music business are soul singers and groups, surely you must agree with me there?'

`Absolutely, wi'out any shadow o' doubt an' if yer bought tickets an' went to a performance by one of em then I'd agree yer've been to a live music event. When all as yer doing is listening to em on record, choose how many other folk are there, yer ant. Surely *you* must agree there, after all, you're the Inspector an' I'm just a lowly Sergeant, you're supposed to be the intelligent one.'

`Okay D.J. you win, I agree a record player and a stack of forty-fives doesn't equate to live music. However, I still find your intolerance of

Northern Soul more than a little puzzling, there's some bloody good songs in the genre.'

`I'm not intolerant of it at all Troy. I just get bored wi it after a bit. I mean, to properly enjoy that type o' music I think yer need to be a dancer, an' as yer can see I'm not exactly built for dancing, on account o' mi Mam's...'

`Yes, yes I know D.J. on account of your Mothers pies, chips, and the occasional pint or ten.'

`Got it in one.'

Detective Sergeant Dean Jacobs smiled and patted his belly as he expertly manoeuvred the car through the narrow gateway into Minneymoor Field and eased to a stop.

`Right then Sergeant, let's have a look, see what we've got here.'

`Right yer are Sir.'

The two policemen instantly reverted to their professional personas as they got out of the car and started to make their way across the field to where the crime scene tape could be seen, fluttering in the breeze.

Detective Inspector Troy Dennis had moved back to his birthplace of Conisborough some four months previously after twenty-five years of living and policing in the North-Eastern town of Blyth. Upon the death of his wife Lynn he had transferred back to South Yorkshire. Although he and Jacobs had only been working together for those few short months the two men had formed a firm friendship. So much so in fact, that Dennis now rented the spare bedroom in his recently divorced Sergeants house. After identifying themselves to the uniformed P.C. guarding the crime scene and donning protective overalls they ducked under the tape.

`Morning Dusty, what delights do you have for us this morning then?' Dennis said.

`Morning Inspector, Sergeant.' The small, white-clad figure of Lydia `Dusty' Duncan turned and smiled a greeting from under her hood. `It's gonna be a slow process this one I'm afraid. Basically, what we've got is the skeletal remains of what appears to be a child, judging by the size of what we've found so far.'

`Skeletal remains? So, whoever it is they've been there some time?'

`Years Inspector. Any more than that I can't say and, to be honest, this branch of forensics isn't exactly my area of expertise. The best I can say for the moment is we'll finish up exhuming the remains, get em back to the lab and I'll give em the once-over. After that any expert analysis will have to come from a forensic archaeologist.'

`You can't give us anything?'

`Nothing worthwhile I'm afraid. I tend to specialise in fresher corpses myself.'

`Yes, so do we. Why do I get the feeling that this is going to be a right pain in the arse for all concerned?'

`Never mind Sir, be a bit boring if every job were an easy one.' Jacobs said.

`Yes D.J. but this is Conisborough for Christs sake and I feel like I've just walked into an episode of CSI or Cold Case or one of those other shitty American shows the wife used to like so much.'

`No, me an' you Sir? We're much more Miami Vice than that. I reckon if I lost a couple o' pounds an' shaved mi beard off, I'd be a dead-ringer for that Don Johnson feller.'

`More Boris Johnson methinks Jacobs. Anyway, let's crack on. Let us know as soon as Dusty, won't you?'

`Will do Inspector, bye now. See yer Sergeant.'

`Catch yer later Dusty.'

****

`First impressions D.J.?' Dennis asked as they made their way back to the car.

`I reckon yer could be right Sir, this one's got the potential to be a right old ball-ache. Pound to a pinch o' shit foul play's involved, unless o' course we've stumbled on some sort o' ancient burial site.'

`Highly unlikely I'm afraid. Where the hell do we start our investigation though? I mean, we don't even have a time frame with which to work.'

`Aye, give me a fresh body an' a smoking gun any day o' week.'

`Right, let's start with missing persons, particularly juveniles, going back, I don't know, twenty years or so?'

`There is one as springs to mind Sir, from even further back.'

`Go on D.J.'

`Do yer remember that young lad as went missing way back in early eighties, Simon something or other? He lived just o'er back o' field, on Bradley Estate.'

`Oh yes. West wasn't it, Simon West? We would've been about the same age. Didn't someone confess at the time?'

`I think so Sir. They never found the lads body though. I were about fifteen at time an' I remember two lads as I were at school wi', the Jennings twins, were questioned at the time cos they'd been wi' him the night before he disappeared. I've had the pair of em in for questioning more than once mesen since, a couple o' wannabe gangsters. My old DCI, Bill Quinn, was on the original investigation.'

`Right, well let's start with young Simon West then but we pull all the files I mentioned, we can't put all our eggs in the same basket after all. You can start that ball rolling when we get back D.J. while I make some enquiries into how much a forensic archaeologist is likely to add to the budget. Before that however, how do you think your mother might feel about feeding two hungry bobbies?'

`Oh, I wouldn't worry too much about that Sir. We won't have to bother mi Mam this morning. Auntie Iris, mi Mams sister, lives just down the road on Taylor Street an' she's just as good a cook as mi Mam.'

`Then please lead the way Sergeant.'

`As yer wish Sir.'

Jacobs started the engine and eased the car out of the gateway.

Chapter 12

10.00 a.m.

`Morning Sis, Logan not about?'

Pete O'Hanlon said brightly as he breezed into the kitchen of his sisters' house.

`He's just nipped out for fags an' milk, he won't be long. What you doing here anyway, what's up wi' work?' Niamh asked.

`I've got used to having Mondays off this last couple o' months so I thought fuck it, no point being gaffer if I can't come an' go as I please. I've just fetched them papers round for our Loge, yer know, them as that Grace bird were on about last night?'

`An' how come she gave em to you, I thought she were gonna drop em off herself?'

`Just thought I'd save her the journey is all, save having to give her directions an' all.'

`So, yer got up this morning an' thought to yerself `I know, I'll just nip over to Clifton an' pick them papers up for mi brother-in-law save everybody else the hassle'?... Oh no... Peter... you didn't?'

`Dint what Sis?' Pete smiled.

`Yer did dint yer? for fucks sake Pete, is no woman safe wi' you? Yer've got no morals at all.'

`I ant done owt wrong, she wanted to, I wanted to, so we did. What's wrong wi' that?'

`She's Uncle Pats daughter, that's what's wrong wi' it.'

`So what? Ave yer never heard o' kissing cousins? We ant done owt illegal.'

`I know you little brother and I bet there was very little kissing involved!'

`Ay up, what's going on here, who ant done owt illegal?' Logan said entering the kitchen.

`This dirty little bastard's only gone an' shagged that Grace as we met in pub last night, that's what's going on.'

`Yer never did...'

`Oh don't you fuckin start an' all mate. Christ Almighty, it weren't planned, we just shared a taxi home from Indian last night. When we got to her place she asked if I fancied coming in for a coffee an' everything else just sort of happened.'

`Come off it Peter, `come in for coffee'? seriously? I bet in that filthy mind o' yours yer were already halfway upstairs before the taxi door had shut. Mind yer, I wouldn't fancy being in your shoes when mi Mam finds out.'

`Hey, come on Niamh, there's no need for yer to go saying owt.'

`Why ever not little brother? After all, yer ant done owt illegal.' Niamh mocked.

`Come on Sis, what she don't know won't hurt her. There's no need to start trouble for no reason.'

`Mebbe not, I'll just ave to try an' make sure it dunt slip out in conversation is all. Right, I'm off down to our Phoebes. I promised I'd watch the twins for a couple o' hours.'

Niamh kissed her husband good bye and was gone.

`Yer a mucky old bastard Hanny.' Logan said and smiled.

`Guilty as charged.'

Pete smiled back and the two men high-fived, laughing like the schoolboy friends they'd once been.

****

An hour later Logan sat alone at the table and pulled the bundle of papers towards him. Pete had stayed long enough for a bacon sandwich, coffee, and a couple of fags before pleading places to be and leaving. Lighting himself another cigarette, Logan decided he would give everything a quick glance over first and return later to the more interesting papers for a more intense perusal.

The first thing of interest that caught his eye was an old audio cassette tape. Logan knew that they had a tape deck somewhere in the house but he'd wait for Niamh to return home rather than waste time looking for it himself. His wife had an uncanny ability to lay her hand straight on any object, no matter how long it had been hidden from view. He himself could quite conceivably empty every cupboard and drawer in the house and still be no nearer to his goal, so he put the tape carefully to one side. Next came a pile of grainy photographs. Most featured Patrick O'Hanlon, who he recognised immediately, with a man who Logan assumed was a young Eric Dalton. In these photographs Pat could always be seen handing over an envelope to Dalton. The remaining images invariably showed Dalton who in each one could be seen counting large sums of money, presumably the contents of the envelopes. Logan turned the photographs over. Written in a black marker pen in bold letters was a date, time, and location. Working quickly, he was soon able to sort the photographs into corresponding pairs. Pat handing over the envelope in one picture, Dalton counting the money in the next, times and dates on the backs matching. There were ten pairs of pictures, taken approximately four months apart, over a period of four years from June nineteen-seventy-eight to July nineteen-eighty-two.

Logan sat back now and lit another cigarette.

` Well, well, well Patrick James O'Hanlon, seems like yer were a naughty boy back in the day. It also seems like yer were a clever, devious, bastard to boot.' He said almost admiringly.

The next document, Logan guessed, was a transcription of what he would hear later on the cassette, so he set this aside also. A quick reading of the letter to Grace from her mother told him nothing he hadn't heard the night before. That left just one more envelope.

Attached to this envelope with a paperclip was a hand-written note.

`I was going to keep this to myself and it is the only one of the papers that I would like you to return. However, after meeting you all last night I feel that it's only right to share it with you. Unfortunately, I can remember nothing of the events your uncle describes, I really wish that I could. Grace x.'

Logan examined the envelope. It was addressed simply `Baby Girl'. Feeling almost as if he was intruding into something private he opened the envelope carefully. Inside was a small colour photograph showing Patrick O'Hanlon holding a young, pretty, curly-haired girl of about three years old and a hand-written letter, the back of the photograph was dated August 1974.

`Darling Baby Girl,

If you are reading this it means either that your mother has decided that the time is right to let you know the truth or (God forbid) We are both now dead and you have found this among her things. I was forty-two-years old by the time you were born on 8th May 1971, a date that will be forever embedded in my heart. Please believe me when I tell you that I loved your mother very much and she loved me but our relationship was not to be. Your parents had already been married for a matter of months before Sylvia and I started our brief affair, the result of which was you Baby Girl.

Our relationship was doomed before ever it started, we both knew that but the attraction we felt for each other dictated that we allowed our hearts to rule our heads, for a few short weeks anyway. By the time we came to our senses and reluctantly ended our affair Sylvia was pregnant with you. For reasons that are not up to me to tell you there is no doubt that you are my daughter and although I have very little time for the man you know as Dad, credit where it's due, when we came clean about our affair he agreed without hesitation to bring you up as his own. Trust me when I say, this was by far the hardest thing that I have ever done in my life.

You're probably wondering about the photograph I enclosed with this letter. Well the big, scruffy-looking bloke with the huge moustache is me, I'm sure you know who the little angel I'm holding is. This was to be the last time I ever held you in my arms as your mother and I had agreed by then that it would be too confusing for you to keep meeting me and from that day I had to make do with watching from afar or the occasional innocent looking meeting.

I hope you might somehow remember the man who would sometimes buy you a bottle of pop and some crisps in the beer garden or give you a couple of pounds to spend on the Catholic Club trips to the seaside. I've been a hard man during a hard life but nothing ever hurt me as much as not being a part of your life and I hope this letter might go some way to explaining why. Please don't hate either me or your mother Baby Girl, we did the things we did with the best of intentions.

I will love you always.

The letter was signed Patrick James O'Hanlon and dated the eighth of May nineteen-eighty-seven, Graces sixteenth birthday.

Logan sat back and removed his reading glasses. That feeling of intruding into somebody else's personal business, albeit with permission, was even stronger now. He thought of his own children and his two grandchildren. It was impossible even to begin to imagine the pain Pat must have felt, to have played no part in the life of his only child must have been heart rending.

Patrick O'Hanlon, like all the men in the family, had been a big, strong man. Logan had always felt however, that the term `gentle giant' could well have been invented with him in mind. That wasn't to say that he had been any sort of soft touch, far from it. In fact, he had been just as handy with his fists and prepared to use them as the rest of the menfolk. No, there was a softer side to Pat that often manifested itself in the company of women and children and in his expert playing of both guitar and banjo. Logan knew that Niamhs sister, Eileen, had been particularly fond of Pat, so much so in fact, that upon his death fourteen years before she had moved into his house and taken over the running of his allotment. Coincidentally she too had never married and was a talented musician.

Logan checked his watch and was surprised to see it was almost twelve-fifteen. Although he had never been the biggest of drinkers he suddenly felt the urge for what Jud always referred to as `a couple o' liveners'.

`Bollocks to it.' He said out loud reaching for his phone. `Niamh? I'm just popping out for a couple o' pints, I'll not be long love. Yeah... yeah, I know it's my turn to cook... no I won't try an' talk yer into avin' Ginos later. Okay, bye.'

He hit the end button and scrolled down to another number.

`Pete, I'm off down Lion for a couple if yer fancy it... okay pal, see yer there.'

Logan ended the call and tidied all the papers away, thinking sadly what a crying shame it had been that Grace had never got to know her real father.

Lighting another cigarette, he picked up his keys and left the house.

Chapter 13

5.30.p.m.

Troy Dennis' Office, CID H.Q. Doncaster.

`Hi Dusty, what have you got for me?'

Troy Dennis leaned back in his chair and propped his feet on the desk in front of him.

`Not much I'm afraid Inspector.' Said the voice at the other end of the line. `I'm just leaving the scene now. We've been working under floodlights for the last hour but I'm fairly confident we've collected all of the remains. They're being transported to the lab as we speak and I'm off home, I'll examine them in the morning. Any luck tracking down an expert?'

` The powers that be have given me the green light to bring one in, some lassie from Dublin, a Doctor Brannigan but unfortunately she can't be with us before next Monday.'

`Brannigan? Would that be Layla Brannigan by any chance?'

`The very same, know her, do you?'

`Only by reputation and I attended a lecture she gave a few years back. She's regarded as one of the best in her field.'

`All very good I'm sure but she could be the last word in forensic archaeology, the fact is she's fuck all good to me in Dublin, pardon my French. Is there no crumb of comfort, no matter how small, that you could throw my way Dusty?'

` I can hazard a guess but that's all it will be Inspector, remember I haven't properly examined any of the remains and as I said earlier, this isn't my area of expertise.'

`I understand that Pet but anything's better than what I have at the minute.'

`That's really quite cute Inspector.'

`What is?'

`You don't do it very often but every now and then you get a slight Geordie twang to your accent... and you just called me pet.'

`Did I? I didn't realise, sorry.'

`No need, like I said, it's cute. I used to like Auf Wiedersehen Pet' when I was young, I had quite a crush on Kevin Whateley as it happens.'

`The bloke who played Neville? I would have thought all the young girls at the time would have gone more for Wayne.'

`Nah, them Cockneys are always too sure of their selves and too loud-mouthed for my liking.'

`Well I suppose that explains your attraction to my Sergeant, D.J. could never be accused of being either.'

`Now there is a fine figure of a man, well worthy of any girls' crush...'

`Dusty please!'

`Well you started it Inspector.' There was the sound of laughter down the line.

`Yes, I suppose I asked for that. Could we please get back to your guesswork now?'

`Okay but I must stress again, this is purely conjecture. From what we've uncovered I'm fairly confident that the remains are those of a young male between ten and twelve years old, possibly older if they were small for their age. There was also some damage to the skull. Anything more than that I'm not prepared to say.'

`Damage?'

`Yeah, the skull displays signs that I'd expect to see in somebody who had suffered some sort of blunt force trauma but I refuse to elaborate further.'

`Okay, thanks anyway. I don't suppose there was anything with the remains that might help with identification like... oh, I don't know, an identity bracelet or a perfectly preserved copy of his birth certificate perhaps?'

`Afraid not Inspector. It looks like you're going to have to do this one the hard way.'

`Yes, just for a change eh? Thanks again Dusty, I'll catch up with you some time tomorrow.'

`Okay Inspector, see you soon.'

Dennis leaned forward again, replaced the handset, and stood up wearily. A quick glance at his watch told him it was now quarter to six. He quickly covered the few paces to the door and opened it.

`D.J. let's call it a day. I need a pint.'

`Right yer are Sir but if yer don't mind me saying, for a man as reckons not to drink during week, yer getting a bit fond o' these after work pints.'

`Yes, I put that down to the influence of my landlord Sergeant.'

`Me Sir?' D.J. asked with mock indignation. `I'm sure I don't know what yer mean.'

`Come on man, let's just grab a couple of beers while we can.'

`Fine by me Sir, fancy a couple in Conyers then, Lion dunt open while seven.'

`Anywhere will do D.J. I'm really not fussy.'

****

`Black Sabbath, Thin Lizzy, A History of The Blues.'

Troy Dennis was searching through the compact discs he had found in the glove compartment of Jacobs' car.

`Who's this though? Paul `Ballo' Ballington? I can honestly say I've never heard of him.'

`One o' mi daughters got me that one for father's day last year. He's a lad from out Dinnington way I think, a plumber by trade. He's a bit like a one-man Barron Knights, yer know, he takes popular tunes an' puts his own lyrics to em. Some of em are really near the knuckle, filthy almost, he's very talented though an' well worth a listen. Stick it on if yer want Troy.'

`Maybe some other time D.J. it's nice to know however, that not everything in your musical collection incorporates screeching guitars.'

`Yer should be able to find some country and western in there if it's easy listening yer after but if it's Northern Soul yer want I'm afraid yer out o' luck.'

`More's the pity. I'm afraid we'll just have to agree to disagree when it comes to music D.J. Pint of Stones and a packet of pork scratchings I presume?'

`That'll be just the ticket Troy.' Jacobs said as he pulled into the car park of The Lord Conyers.

Chapter 14

7.15.p.m.

Minneymoor Lane, Conisborough.

From his position, standing at the end of his drive, Henry Dutton watched the last of the police vehicles pull off the field and head slowly up the lane each one crawling in a forlorn attempt to avoid the many potholes. More than fifty years he'd lived on this lane and never in all that time could it have been described as much more than a dirt track.

For the last thirty-five of those fifty-odd years he had lived in fear of this day. It must be the West boy, he thought, after all this time they'd finally found him. Would the police now be able to work out what had really happened all those years ago? Would they soon be calling at his door to make him answer for his actions that Summer? What could they actually do to an old man just three weeks short of his eighty-third birthday anyway. Happen I'd rather not find out, he thought as he made his way slowly to his front door.

****

Two hours later Henry made his way upstairs, carefully balancing a tray upon which were two mugs of cocoa. He eased his way into the bedroom where his wife lay in bed awaiting him.

`Henry, is that you?'

Doreen Dutton looked towards the door with sightless eyes, cataracts having robbed her of her vision in recent years.

`Of course love. Who else would it be?' Henry said, placing the tray on the bedside table.

`I wasn't sure if it might not be Derek come to say goodnight. He usually does you know.'

`Now, now love, you know that's not true, our Derek hasn't lived here for years. He emigrated to Australia a long time ago.'

`I know that Henry, I'm not stupid you know but it doesn't change the fact that he usually comes to wish me goodnight, unless of course he's too busy with work.'

`Aye sorry lass, I keep forgetting.' Henry sighed sadly.

Not only had his beloved Doreen lost her sight, in recent years she had also developed dementia and conversations like this one were becoming increasingly common. He helped his wife to sit up in bed, making sure she was comfortable, before carefully placing the mug in her hands.

`Here yer go love, drink this up. I've even put us a little tot o' rum in it, just to keep the cold away o' course.'

`Ooh, that were lovely.' Doreen said a few minutes later, as she allowed her husband to take the mug from her and ease her back down in the bed. `I'm feeling very tired now Henry. Do me a favour love? Tell Derek he needn't look in on me tonight, I'll be fine until morning.'

`Of course my love, sweet dreams.' Henry kissed his wifes forehead gently.

Within seconds Doreen Dutton was snoring gently. Henry was surprised how quick and easy it was. He placed the pillow over his wifes face and pressed down. There was no struggle, the only movement being a slight stiffening of the body towards the end. Within moments the sounds of snoring had ceased and his wife lay still. Henry removed the pillow and stepped back from the bed.

`I'm sorry Doreen love but believe me, it's for the best.'

****

Half an hour later Henry finished his glass of whiskey and placed the empty tumbler on the kitchen table.

`Reyt, let's get this over with Henry lad.' He said out loud.

Calmly, he reached to the side of his chair and retrieved a heavy-duty plastic bag, which he quickly placed over his head and secured round his neck with a large cable tie. He then dipped his hands into the bowl of cooking oil he had placed on the table earlier. God forgive me, he thought before leaning back in his chair and breathing deeply.

Chapter 15

Monday 16th January 2017, 9.00 a.m.

Troy Dennis' office, Doncaster CID.

`Inspector Dennis, I presume. My name's Layla Brannigan, I believe you're expecting me.'

A tall, good-looking woman walked in through the open office door, smiling and right hand extended in greeting.

`Actually no Miss. I'm Sergeant Jacobs, the Boss is with the Chief Constable just now. He shouldn't be long afore he's back though.'

Dean Jacobs took the proffered hand in his own and shook it, pleasantly surprised at the firmness of the woman's grip.

`Can I offer you a cup of coffee Miss Brannigan? Don't worry it's not the usual station slop, Inspector Dennis insists on taking his from that thing.' Jacobs indicated the state-of-the-art coffee-maker that took up one corner of the small office. `Apparently, I can offer yer Latte, Americano, Espresso, Cappuccino, or even a Chocó-Mocha, whatever the bloody hell one o' them is.'

`A Latte would be lovely, thank you Sergeant and please call me Layla, Miss Brannigan makes me feel like someone's maiden-aunt.'

`Right yer are Layla, one Latte coming up an' you can call me D.J. everybody else does. Please tell me yer were named after the song.'

`As near as makes no difference D.J. I was actually conceived after an Eric Clapton concert in the seventies, if I'd been born a boy I would have been named after the great man himself. Are you a fan yourself?'

`Oh yes, anybody with any musical taste has to admire old `Slow Hand'. To be honest though, mi own personal favourite has to be Gary Moore, he just had something extra in my opinion.'

`I agree D.J. I was lucky enough to be there the night he played that tribute concert for Phil Lynott in Dublin, a superb performance.'

`I've got that on DVD at home. I managed to see him at Sheffield City Hall a couple o' years afore he died, one o' the best gigs I've ever been to.'

`What's that D.J.?'

Troy Dennis breezed into the office and flopped down into his chair.

`Nowt as you'd be interested in Sir. I was just discussing music with Miss Brannigan h...'

`I do apologise Doctor Brannigan, Troy Dennis.' He said, jumping to his feet and offering his hand. `I'm sorry, I just didn't see you there, walking around in a world of my own. I wasn't expecting you until this evening.'

`No problem Inspector. I actually flew in late last night and after a fine breakfast in my hotel this morning thought there was no time like the present to get started. I must admit I'm quite eager to see the remains you've found. With all the lectures I give these days I don't often get the chance to get my hands dirty, so to speak.'

`Well I have to admit, you're not here a moment too soon Doctor.'

`Please Inspector, call me Layla, I do hate formality. If you could point me in the direction of the morgue I'd like to get cracking. I'm sure you've got plenty to do yourself.'

`I can do better than that Layla. The good Sergeant here will escort you there himself and introduce you to our esteemed pathologist. He and Dusty are after all quite an item, eh D.J.?'

`Aww come on Sir, leave it out will yer?' Jacobs mumbled, blushing furiously.

`Now, now Sergeant no need to be shy about these things is there? Dusty is a lovely lass, is she not?'

`Aye, she is that Sir. If yer'd like to follow me Layla.'

`Certainly D.J. See you later Inspector, excellent coffee by the way. I think I'll get one of those machines for my office back in Dublin.'

`I wouldn't be without mine and it's Troy. Goodbye Layla.'

****

`So, is there any truth in what the Inspector was saying back there or was he just winding you up?' Layla asked a few moments later.

`Me an' Dusty? That's Lydia Duncan, the pathologist. Aye, we've been seeing each other for a few weeks now.'

`Is it serious?'

`I'm not sure, she's a cracking lass an' we have a good laugh an' that.'

`But...?'

`Oh, I don't know, look at me. I'm fifty-year-old, top side o' eighteen stone, grey. She's thirty-eight an' pretty as a picture, what the hell can she see in me?'

`Does she share your taste in music or anything?'

`Oh aye an' she likes rugby an' all. In fact, we're off to an open-mic night in Mexborough tonight, I've got a bit of a surprise for her an' all.'

`Then I'm sure you've nothing to worry about.'

`Aye, yer probably right lass, just me being daft as usual.'

****

4.30 p.m.

Troy Dennis' Office.

As had been the case earlier, Dennis, Jacobs, and Layla were all present in the small office. This time however, they had been joined by Dusty, who was standing by the coffee-machine, nursing a Cappuccino, Dennis and Layla were seated at the desk. Dean Jacobs had adopted his customary position, standing by the door.

`I've got to say that it's been a very interesting day so far.' Layla was saying now. `Dusty's done a first-class job, both in excavating and reconstructing the remains and her initial, educated, guesswork was fairly accurate as well.'

At this Layla nodded over to Dusty and smiled, who raised her mug in salute.

`All in a days' work for `Team Dennis'.' She smiled back.

`Team Dennis', very catchy I must say.'

`It's a vast improvement on `The Blackleg Brigade' at least, which was the alternative.' Dennis said.

`Oh I don't know Sir, I quite liked `Troys Troops' mesen.' Laughed Jacobs from the door.

`Please, don't think we've lost our minds Layla, let me explain. They were all names jokingly put forward by the members of our small team here at H.Q. After successfully concluding a major investigation at the end of last year, the powers that be decided to form a small, I suppose you'd call it a task force, comprising of; myself in charge, D.J. as my able second-in-command, and two Detective Constables, Andy Gibbons and Lisa Carter. Our remit being that we would, alongside all our other duties, take a slightly more in-depth involvement in any major inquiry as and when the top brass deems it appropriate. Dusty here was, by mutual consent of the team, given an honorary status as a full member.'

`I see, a sort of `Major Crimes Elite'. I must say, I think `The Blackleg Brigade' is my favourite. What does `Blackleg' allude to by the way?'

`It was the nickname given to the inquiry by the press when it became public knowledge that the perpetrators painted the legs of their victims.' Dennis informed her.

`Really? How very intriguing, you'll have to tell me more about it sometime. Anyway, as I was saying, I've spent today examining the remains and what we have is indeed the skeleton of a young adult male between the ages of ten and twelve years old. The remains themselves have been interred for a period of somewhere between thirty to forty years. At this point let me tell you that it's unusual, not unheard of, but unusual all the same to find as complete a skeleton after such a long time. Only a few of the smaller bones were unaccounted for.'

`Why's it so unusual?' D.J. asked.

`Without boring you with a long-winded explanation of the stages of decomposition, suffice it to say that one would expect that the smell of putrefaction emanating from a shallow-grave, such as the one we're interested in, would attract the attentions of scavengers, such as foxes and the like. In some cases, a fox has been known to detach a human head from the corpse and carry it away.'

`The area the body was found in had, until recent weeks, been covered in dense overgrowth and had been for many years. Do yer think that could explain it?'

`Possibly. The cause of death was undoubtedly blunt force trauma to the front of the skull. It's my professional opinion that the body was laid on its back and then bludgeoned several times, more than likely with a medium sized rock of some description.'

`Jesus Christ, the poor little bastard.' Jacobs said, shaking his head sadly.

`There were some other injuries to the body, most notably a healed fracture to the left tibia suggesting an accident during infancy, which could be of some help to you in identifying the remains. The bones in both hands showed extensive damage, more than likely administered in the same manner as the fatal blows to the head. We can only hope that the poor child was either unconscious or already deceased before these injuries were inflicted. I've also taken some samples which can be sent off for DNA analysis. I can pull a few strings and request a fast-tracking of the results if or when you have something to compare them with but it will still take a few days at least before anything comes back from the lab.'

`Is that even possible after all these years?' Dennis asked now.

`There's nothing there that'll help you catch his killer Troy but if you have any ideas as to who our young boy could be, then a DNA comparison with a living relative will give you a positive identification.'

`Bloody amazing what they can do these days. It's hard to believe it would be possible after being buried for thirty-odd years.' Jacobs said in awe.

`It is impressive D.J. but that's nothing compared with those bones they found last year in a farmers' field in France. A DNA comparison with one of his great-nephews was able to positively identify the remains as those of Private Henry Parker, who died more than one hundred years ago during the Battle of the Somme.'

`Christ, I knew DNA were useful but I had no idea they could do stuff like that with it.'

`Have you got any ideas as to who the mystery boy might be?' Layla asked.

`There are a couple of possibilities but the one that stands out is a young lad by the name of Simon West who disappeared back in July nineteen-eighty-two. He was last seen leaving home which was just a few minutes' walk from where the body was found.' Dennis answered.

`Have you tried matching dental records?'

`Non-existent I'm afraid. According to his older sister, who has spent the last twenty-five years living in New York, their parents both had a morbid fear of the dentist and refused to inflict any dental procedures on their offspring.'

`Where are the parents now?'

`Both deceased, unfortunately. The father was killed in a work-related accident a couple of years after the boy disappeared. The mother was committed to a mental institution just before her daughter emigrated, she died there four years ago. To be perfectly honest the daughter, Nicola Fearns as she's called now, struck me as being quite a cold fish. Gave the impression of being seriously inconvenienced by my questions and totally uninterested that we may or may not have found her brother. Apparently, there was also a younger brother, Anthony, black sheep of the family according to her ladyship, left home in eighty-nine when he was sixteen and none of the family ever heard from him again. We're trying to trace him but he could be anywhere, literally.'

`Are there any other living relatives, preferably male, who could provide a sample?'

`None that we're aware of but we'll keep looking.'

`Well, if all else fails I could attempt a facial reconstruction on the skull. I must warn you however, that it's a time consuming and costly procedure. You'd be far better tracing the brother and asking him to supply a sample for comparison.'

`Right, well that's enough for one day. The good Sergeant here and his delightful companion have insisted that I accompany them to some

God-awful rock concert tonight. Why do I let them talk me into these things? I don't even like heavy metal.'

`It's not a concert *or* a heavy metal gig. It's just an open mic night, yer'll enjoy it if yer go wi' an open mind.' Jacobs laughed. `In fact, why don't you join us Layla? I've got a funny feeling it could be right up your street.'

`I'd love to D.J. but I don't think I'll have time to get myself ready and organise a taxi to get myself there at such short notice.'

`No need for all that.' Dusty piped-up. `We'll swing by your hotel now and pick up your stuff, you can get ready at mine. You can have my spare room tonight as well and I'll bring you in in the morning.'

`Well, if you're sure...'

`That's settled then, come on. See yer there about half-seven Big Lad.' Dusty pecked Jacobs on the cheek and left with Layla in tow.

`Reyt, we'd best be off an' all Troy. Taxi's picking us up at seven from our place an' we want to look us best for the girls, don't we?'

`What have I let myself in for?' moaned Dennis. `Lead the way Sergeant.'

****

7.45 p.m.

Mexborough Athletic Club

`I feel like a proper prick D.J. I understand entirely that this is hardly a shirt and tie affair but did you really have to dress me up like a roadie for Status Bastard Quo? And look at yourself man, all you're missing is a bandana and you could pass as a member of the Conisborough Chapter of the Hells Angels. How the fuckin hell does this equate to, and I quote, `looking our best for the girls' and that's another thing...'

`Give it a rest Troy will yer? yer look great. Look around, yer don't look out o' place. In fact, it suits yer down to ground mate.'

Troy Dennis was dressed in jeans, white trainers, a plain black t-shirt and a denim jacket, Jacobs having insisted earlier that a sports coat would be unacceptable attire for this evening. For his own part, D.J. had opted for jeans, cowboy boots, a Lynyrd Skynyrd `Freebird' t-shirt, and to complete the outfit, a black leather waistcoat.

`Eyes front Troy lad, here comes Girl school.'

`Eh? Good God...'

Dusty and Layla were standing in the doorway of the concert room obviously looking for the two detectives. Both were dressed in almost identical outfits of stonewashed jeans, boots and biker-style leather jackets. Dusty smiled and waved as she finally caught Jacobs' eye.

`*Inspector Dennis!!* My, you do look the part.' She said as the two women joined them.

`Well, I feel like a complete idiot. Anyway, let me get you ladies a drink. What will it be?'

`Just half a lager for me, thanks.'

`I'll have a Jack Daniels and coke please if that's alright.'

`Not a problem. Another pint D.J.?'

`Aye, please Troy. Do yer need a hand?'

`No, no, I'll be fine. You keep the ladies entertained. This is certainly more your scene than mine.'

Ninety minutes and three drinks later, Dennis' mood had improved considerably.

`Well I've got to hand it to you D.J. I'm enjoying this far more than I thought I would. I think that last band was far superior to the first though.'

`Aye, yer not wrong Troy but yer in for a real treat now. Mi brother used to play with these lads up until a couple o' years back. Get ready to rock everyone.'

Jacobs nodded towards the stage, where two men were strapping on guitars while a third took his place behind the drum kit. Three songs later the twenty or so people present were applauding wildly.

`Thank you so much everyone.' The lead guitarist and singer was saying now. `Ladies and gents it's now special guest time. We have in our midst this evening a guitarist of sublime talent who has very kindly offered to join us for a couple o' numbers. So, without further ado, please give a warm welcome to our old mate, `Big Deano Jacobs'.'

`Be back in a bit. Get us another beer in will yer Troy?' and with a quick wink at his speechless companions D.J. strolled confidently towards the stage.

`Reyt then boys an' girls...' he said into the microphone as he slung a guitar over his shoulder. `... I'm a bit out o' practice so I hope this goes okay. Just a couple o' songs, the first one's by Gary Moore an' then we're gonna do an Eric Clapton number. Hope yer like em.'

****

`Well, you're a dark horse and no mistake. You told me that was your brothers' guitar back at the house.' Dennis said when Jacobs had re-joined them.

`Aye, it is an' that's our kids' old band an' all but who do yer think taught the little twat to play in first place?'

`Well I for one am extremely impressed.' Said a jubilant Dusty, throwing her arms round his neck and planting a big kiss on his lips. `That was amazing, I can't believe you never mentioned it before.'

`I wanted it to be a surprise.'

`Well it was certainly that and you played and sang `Wonderful Tonight' as well as I've ever heard it before. I just wish I'd thought to film it for my Dad.' Layla said.

`I must admit, I enjoyed mesen up there. It must be four years or more since I played to any kind of crowd.'

`Well don't leave it so long next time D.J. you were superb.' Troy shook his hand smiling. `The Singing Sergeant', though it's beyond me how you play so well with those stubby fingers. Well done mate, well done.'

Chapter 16

Tuesday 17th January 2017, 7.30 a.m.

`I don't know how you do it D.J. I mean, look at you man, you had just as much to drink as I did last night but I'm as rough as a bears' arse and you look like as though all you did was spend a night in front of the telly.'

`Well, if it weren't for fact I'm such a fat fucker, I'd put it down to a high metabolism, as it is I reckon I'm just lucky, I've never suffered wi' hangovers.'

`Believe you me, I'm suffering enough for the pair of us.'

`It were a cracking night though, yer've got to admit.'

`Yes, I'll give you that, I thoroughly enjoyed myself. I didn't reckon much to that last lot though.'

`Aye, they weren't much cop reyt enough but they're only young lads, they've plenty time to grow out o' that death metal phase, it's not everybody's cup o' tea.'

`No, and a cup of tea isn't going to help matters either. A double Espresso's what I need and that's just for starters.'

`Here we are Troy, not be long now.'

Jacobs pulled into the car park at H.Q. and eased into an available parking space.

`Right, I'm not to be disturbed until I've had my caffeine fix.' Dennis said getting out of the car. `Even if the bloody Home Secretary herself comes-a-calling.'

`Right yer are Sir.'

`Oh... and Sergeant?'

`Yes Sir?'

`Lose the bloody earring. If the Chief Constable sees that she'll have a coronary.'

`Right yer are again Sir.' Jacobs smiled sheepishly and reached up to his left ear to remove the large gold sleeper.

****

Twenty minutes later, caffeine levels satisfactorily replenished, Dennis stood in front of his team.

`...right you lovely lot, that brings you all up to speed on what little we've learned since last we met. Any questions?'

Detective Constable Lisa Carter raised her hand.

`Not a question Sir, more an update of my own.'

`Go on Lisa.'

`I couldn't sleep last night so I decided to check my e-mails. Well, I read the mail you sent out yesterday evening, yer know updating everybody? When I got to the bit about the old tibia fracture on the remains I checked the time, which was eleven-thirty by the way, did the maths and realised it would only be six-thirty p.m. in New York. I put a call through to Nicola Fearns, the uppity bitch. It turns out that Simon West did indeed break his leg as a toddler, fell down the cellar stairs at his grandparents' house apparently. It's not conclusive I know but it pretty much confirms the remains as those of Simon West I'd say.'

`I'd have to agree. Excellent work Lisa. Keep trying to find the brother though, a DNA sample from him would save us a lot of trouble getting a positive i.d. Anybody else?'

`I'm not sure yer gonna like this Sir.' Andy Gibbons said now.

`Don't worry Andy, I'm not usually in the habit of shooting the messenger, please continue.'

`Are we absolutely certain that cause of death was a blunt trauma injury?'

`That's the conclusion of our highly qualified and expensive expert yes.'

`See, the thing is Sir as yer know, the police at the time got a conviction for Simon Wests murder, albeit without a body.'

`Yes, I know, a confession I believe. What of it?'

`Well, the lad as confessed, one Brian Sutton, claimed that he'd buggered the boy an' then stabbed him `ten or twenty times', his words.'

There was a moment of stunned silence amongst the team at this revelation.

`Oh that's just fucking marvellous!' Dennis exploded now. `For almost thirty seconds I allowed myself to believe we were close to putting this one to bed with relative ease then, in the blink of an eye, we've got a thirty-five year-old murder inquiry on our hands again.'

`I did say yer wouldn't like it Sir.'

`Oh, it's not your fault Andy, it's a right kick in the bollocks but it's not your fault. Oh my God! Not only have we got the coldest of cold cases to investigate but we're also in the unenviable position of proving our predecessors royally fucked up in the first place. Isn't life just a bowl of fucking cherries?'

`Where's this Brian Sutton now? Still in custody I take it?' Jacobs said from the doorway, in an attempt to instil order once again.

`He was committed to Rampton Secure Hospital in early eighty-three, he's been there ever since. I called em last week, when we first discovered the remains, to see if anybody there could get him to confirm where he'd buried the West boys' body. Hit a brick wall I'm afraid, he's always steadfastly refused to reveal what he did with the lad.'

`Right, get back on to Rampton, make an appointment for D.J. and I to see the director, or whatever the top banana there's called, with an option to interview Sutton. Don't let them piss you about Andy, today if possible, tomorrow at the latest.' A much calmer Dennis said now.

`I'll get on to it right away, if we're done here Sir?'

`Yes... and good work Andy, well spotted. Right, that's about it I think. Let me know straight away about the Rampton situation, anything else, unless it's of earth-shattering importance, can wait until tomorrows' briefing.'

****

`I've had a nasty feeling about this case right from that first morning last week D.J. and now it looks like I'm about to be proved right. Christ, what a mess.'

`Aye, I know what yer mean Sir. It could end up opening a right can o' bastard worms this. As if South Yorkshire Police ant had enough bad press in recent times, looks like we're gonna be highlighting another fuck-up.'

`Never rains but it pours, eh mate? I want everything from the original investigation re-examining, there might be something of use to us. Other than that, I have to confess D.J., I'm not sure what our best plan of action might be.'

`I've been thinking about that mesen Sir. Remember I told yer my old DCI was on the original team? Well, I thought as maybe I could pay him a visit, pick his brains so to speak, he might remember summat as could be useful.'

`It's certainly worth a try D.J., although he might not take too kindly to have his past career called into question.'

`The way I see it, he ant got much choice, it's gonna happen any road. Anyway, you don't know Bill Quinn Sir. He were a proper stand up sort o' copper. If he'd fucked up he'd want to know, believe me.'

`Where is he now?'

`He retired about five years back but he's a creature of habit is Bill. He always had a passion for classic motorbikes. Unless he's changed, on any given day yer'll find him in his garage working on his babies, at least until opening time any road.'

`I'll let you handle that then D.J., he might be more forthcoming if we keep it on a more informal basis, so to speak...'

`Eleven a.m. tomorrow morning Sir.' Andy Gibbons poked his head round the office door. `The director at Rampton won't be able to see you himself but he's arranged for Suttons original case worker and his present one to be available. Also, he's got no objections to you interviewing the patient if you think it necessary.'

`Nice one Andy, thanks.'

`That's settled it then D.J., we don't need to be in Retford before tomorrow morning so you can use today to track down your old gaffer and see if he can shed any light on things for us.'

`No problem Sir. I'll meet yer back here later then?'

`Yes. I'd like to say that I was going for a lie-down in a nice quiet corner. Unfortunately though, I think I'd better pay our delightful Chief Constable a visit and let her know the shit's on collision course with the air-conditioning. Wish me luck because, unlike yours truly, she has actually been known to shoot messengers!'

`Oh I don't know Sir, I think she's got quite a soft spot for you really.'

`Yes, I'm reliably informed it's a shallow grave down by the river somewhere.'

****

11.a.m.

Judcars, Denaby Main.

`Ay up Grandma, what brings you down here?' Callum O'Hanlon looked up from his desk smiling.

`It's a taxi I'm after and I thought I'd kill two birds with the one stone by coming here.'

Katie O'Hanlon pulled out a chair and sat facing her grandson.

`How do yer mean?'

`Well, seeing how my first-born grandchild never comes to see me anymore, I decided to come to him. A bit like that Mohammed feller and his mountain.'

`I was round yours for mi dinner last week Grandma.'

`That was tree weeks ago as well you feckin' know. For all you know your poor old Grandfather and me might be lying dead in our bed, the flies and rats making a feast of the two of us.'

`I'm sorry Grandma but things've been reyt busy here just o' late an…'

`And I suppose you've been too busy to be seeing that young Shelley, or whatever this weeks' floozy might be called. For the love o' God, you're your fathers' son and no mistake. I only have to feckin look at you and I'm reminded of all the heartache a son puts his mother through.'

`Aww, come on Grandma. I'm not that bad a lad an' I promise I'll start and come round more often in future.'

`Well, you just mind you do. Now, about this taxi...'

`I won't have owt for about ten or fifteen minutes.'

`Will you stop feckin interrupting me and listen! I don't want it for today, it's Friday I'm after booking it for.'

`Yer should o' said...'

`I did say! If you'd shut that great mouth of yours an' feckin listen to me we might actually get somewhere. Right, that's better. Now, myself, Eileen, and Niamh need to be at Doncaster railway station to catch the twenty-past-eleven train to York. Young Grace, that's your Uncle Patricks' daughter, who we only met last week, as you'd know if you could be bothered coming to see me now and again. Anyway, Grace will be catching the same train when it leaves London. The four of us are going to spend the weekend shopping and having a drink or two. So we need one of those people carrying things to fit the cases in and get us to town on time.'

`That won't be a problem but why don't yer just book a taxi to York an' save all that pissing about wi' trains. It won't cost yer owt either.'

`And how do we meet Grace on the train then yer feckin eejit? Anyway, your Grandfathers' paying for the tickets and I've insisted on going first-class. It's not often he spends his money on me, so I intend to make the most of it.'

`Is he stumping-up the shopping money as well?'

`He feckin will be next month when he gets the credit card bill.' Katie cackled. `And while we're talking about money, would you have a ten pound note for these two fives, I refuse to carry that man about in my purse any longer.'

`What man?'

`That feckin Churchill, that's who.'

`What have yer got against Churchill? He was one of the greatest leaders in history.'

`Winston Churchill, as you'd know if ever you took any interest in your roots was one of those responsible for sending the Auxiliaries and the Black and Tans into Ireland and all the misery that came with them.'

`Oh, right but the Queen's on all the other notes an' coins anyway. Dunt that rile yer just as much?'

`Ah that poor woman, a life of privilege she might have led but she's had it rough also. Didn't me heart go out to her a few years ago when she had the horrible anus and all that. Anyway, didn't she meet Martin a couple of times and shake hands with him to show there were no hard feelings and to apologise.'

`I don't think she apologised Grandma.'

`Of course she did, they just wouldn't report it for fear of looking weak. Anyway, we're all set for Friday then? Right, I'll be away then. Good bye Callum and don't be long in coming to see me now.'

`Bye Grandma.' Callum sat back in his chair, shaking his head in amazement.

They broke the mould when they made that woman, he thought.

Chapter 17

11.45 a.m.

Sprotbrough.

Dean Jacobs watched from the car as the old man lovingly polished the old motorcycle. Retirement certainly seems to suit you, he thought, I just hope I'm not about to piss all over yer chips. Sighing, he opened the door and manoeuvred his bulky frame from the seat.

`Excuse me Sir, Sergeant Jacobs, Doncaster CID. I'm sorry to bother you but we've had reports of a number of thefts of old motorbikes and I couldn't help but notice...'

`Sergeant! Sergeant! Who in the name of Christ would make a fat, incompetent arsehole like you a fuckin Sergeant.' The old man smiled warmly. `And, for your information, this is not an old motorbike. This mi old cocker is a *classic motorcycle*. A nineteen-fifty-four Triumph Bonneville T100 no less but you're right, what I paid for this little beauty was daylight robbery. Not my fault the fuckin clown didn't have a clue what she was worth, I could sell her tomorrow an' nearly double mi money if I wanted.'

`In that case Sir, I'm afraid I'm going to have to ask you to accompany me to the station...'

`Cut the bollocks D.J., just let me get out of these overalls and lock the garage, then we'll go an' get a brew. It's warmer in the house. By the Christ lad, it's good to see yer but summat tells me this int just a social call. Never mind though, all that can wait till we're settled inside. I'll not be a sec.'

Ten minutes later the two former colleagues were drinking large mugs of tea and warming themselves in front of the log fire in retired Detective Superintendent Bill Quinn's' living room.

`Well, I would offer you a seat D.J. mi old son but unless yer've changed this past few years…'

`I'm fine standing thanks Sir.'

`Aye, I thought as much. I only ever saw yer sit down to either eat or drive but if yer gonna insist on leaning on mantelpiece, just make sure yer don't knock any o' them ornaments off. The wife would kill the pair of us afore yer could blink.'

`How is Mrs. Quinn Sir?' Jacobs took three careful steps away from the fireplace.

`Oh, yer know, same as ever, always off on some crusade or other. She's at her sisters in Sheffield at the moment, trying to stop the council from chopping down any more trees. Been there since Friday, the dozy old cow. Last week she was waging a one-woman-vendetta against diesel cars, something she'd seen on telly about all the harmful emissions they produce. Posting leaflets through the doors of every diesel owner in the village, chastising them for damaging the environment she was. It took me two days to convince her I'd converted all mi bikes to run on green fuel before she took a hammer to the lot. I'm thinking of mentioning mi concerns about the melting polar ice-caps in the hopes the silly bitch might piss off to Antarctica or somewhere an' gi' me a bit o' peace.'

`I don't believe yer for a minute, yer wunt be wi'out her Sir.'

`Aye, yer probably reyt lad. A dopey cow she might be but she's my dopey cow all the same. Any road, that's not why yer came here is it lad? What can I do for yer son?'

`Yer've probably heard about them remains as we found in Conisborough last Monday? Well, we're almost certain they're those of Simon West, a young lad who disappeared nigh on thirty-five years ago.'

`Aye, I'm well aware who Simon West is D.J., it was the last big case I worked on with old Cedric Short, my old DCI, yer might remember me going on about him sometimes.'

`Sometimes! I don't think a day went by when yer dint mention him. It were like he were the benchmark against which all other coppers were to be measured.'

`Aye, he more than likely was. Cedric Short was far and away the best bobby I ever worked with. Do yer know he had a success rate second to none when it came to solving major crimes?'

`I certainly do, yer told me at least once a week, every week, for best part of eleven years.' Jacobs laughed.

`I did used to go on a bit I suppose.' Quinn smiled. `Anyway, what is it about these remains that brings yer to my door?'

`As I understand it Sir, yer got a conviction for the boys' murder at the time on the basis of a confession.'

`That's right D.J., some fuckin retard by the name of Sutton. I remember getting a right old bollocking off `The Old Man' cos I went to chin the little bastard when he started bragging about what he'd done to that lad.'

`Do yer remember owt else about his confession?'

`It wasn't beaten out of him if that's what yer mean D.J. Is that what this is all about? Is that little gob-shite making some kind of allegations...?'

`No it's nowt like that at all Sir. If yer could just humour me for a bit, it'll all come clear.'

`Alright then. We'd got the lad bang to rights for killing his step-father and, as I recall, we were almost ready for calling it a night when, out of the blue, he just confesses to killing the young West lad as well. The thing as really got to me though, the reason I went for the little bastard, was he kept on saying how he'd given the boy a `good fucking' before he stabbed him. They were his words `I gave him a good fucking first'. Proper turned my stomach D.J.'

`I can imagine. He definitely said as he'd stabbed the lad though?'

`Absolutely, said he'd stabbed him ten or twenty times an' slit his throat an' all.'

`That brings me to the reason I'm here. See, the thing is, the remains we've unearthed an' we're ninety-nine per-cent sure they're Simon Wests, well they've been examined an' there's absolutely no doubt that the cause of death was a number of blows to the head. I got confirmation before I left the station, the remains show no indication of a knife being used. Apparently, an attack such as Sutton described would've left some marks on the bones. The only injuries present were the fatal blows to the head and the bones in both hands were crushed. I don't know how to tell yer this Sir but it seems like yer might've got the wrong man.'

`Brian Sutton caved his step-fathers' head in wi' a poker before stabbing him to make sure he was dead, mebbe he did same wi' young lad.'

`Then why say as he'd stabbed him then?'

`Dunt make any sense at all does it? Listen, are you in any rush to get away D.J.? What I mean is, can yer spare another half hour or so?'

`Can't see as that'd be a problem. Do yer mind if I ask why?'

`There's summat as I want to show yer, it might end up being some use to yer but it'll take me a bit to find it. Tell yer what, you make us another brew an' I'll be as quick as I can.'

Fifteen minutes later Bill Quinn returned to the living room carrying a large box file that he placed carefully on the coffee table, before taking a drink from his mug and grimacing.

`Nowt worse than cold tea. Don't suppose I can tempt yer into trying summat a bit stronger lad, I've got a cracking little single-malt?' He said as he made his way to the sideboard.

`Not while I'm on duty thanks Sir.'

`Suit yerself but I think I'll just ave a small one. In fact, bollocks to it, I might as well treat mesen.'

Bill Quinn poured himself a very generous measure before returning to his seat.

`Reyt lad, afore I open that box an' show yer what's inside there's a couple o' things yer need to know. First off, Cedric Short never believed as Sutton did for West lad. He said as it dint feel right but we'd got a confession an' the powers that be were happy to go wi' it. Truth be known, I were never hundred per-cent convinced he'd done it mesen but he'd confessed an' he were even able to describe what the lad were wearing at the time so I probably ignored any doubts I might've had. Anyway, a couple o' weeks later `The Old Man' retired. We had a big leaving do for him at his golf club an' him an' his wife went off to live in Cotswolds, happy ever after an' all that bollocks. To cut a long story short, happy ever after lasted about ten years, Mrs. Short collapsed an' died on golf course one morning out o' blue. `The Old Man' couldn't face living down there wi'out her so he sold up an' came back to Doncaster an' that's when all this started.' He patted the box-file. `Let me be quite clear on this D.J., there's nowt in this file as would ever pass as evidence. In fact, a lot of it, as much as it pains me to say it, probably amounts to nothing more than the ramblings of an old man who just couldn't let go.'

`Couldn't let go of what?'

`The job in general I suppose but young Simon West in particular. I told yer he never believed Sutton had killed the lad. In his eyes therefore, that meant there was a murderer walking free. I think while his wife was alive he was determined to enjoy their retirement but once she'd gone well, it must've just started eating away at him again. Like I said, he sold up and moved back home. Any road, every now an' again I'd met up wi' him for a drink an' yer could guarantee he'd bring it up `I never liked him for it Bill' he'd say or `I put the wrong man away'. About ten years ago I got a phone call off one of his sons. The old man was on his last legs in hospital an' he'd been asking for me, would I mind going to see him? Obviously, I said I'd go see him the first chance I got. The next day I'm in this private room in hospital `I'm not long for this world Bill' he says `When I'm gone I've arranged for some files to be sent to you, promise me you'll look through them, put right what we did wrong. We got the wrong man Bill, we got the wrong man' an' his fingers were digging into mi arm till it hurt. `Course I'll check it out boss' I says an' this seemed to cheer him up a bit so we had a chat about old times for an hour an' then said our goodbyes. He died the next morning an' that box was delivered here about a week later.'

`So, what's actually in it?'

`Papers son, what seems like reams an' reams o' bloody papers. Most of it reads like an attempt at writing his memoirs but somewhere in that little lot, when yer find it, is a letter he wrote to me. Well, I say a letter but there's actually pages an' pages o' the bastard thing. Any road, in this letter he goes on again about the West case an' how he's convinced we got it wrong all those years back. To be honest, he probably puts forward a case for reasonable doubt as far as Sutton being responsible goes but there's also a lot of fanciful theories in it as well. He even goes as far as making a number of veiled allegations against some former colleagues but like I said, there's no evidence in anything he wrote. Take it all with yer anyway lad, there just might be summat of use to yer. Who knows, mebbe the old bastard were reyt all along?'

`Well, owt's better than nowt, as mi old Mam likes to say. We'll give em a good looking over an' I'll get em back to yer as soon as.'

`No rush lad. I've read all that's there, some of it more than once. I just hope as yer find summat, as much for old Cedrics' sake as owt else. Now then, when did yer finally pass that Sergeants' exam? Yer must've blown it what, three times afore I retired?'

`Four actually Sir, I passed at mi fifth attempt about four years back.'

`I would o' pissed it mesen, I passed first time back in eighty-one when it were a sight harder. You younguns never had all that legislation bollocks wi' bookies an' scrapyards an' all other shit to contend wi'...'

`Aye that's as maybe but it stood me in good stead for Inspectors' exam, I sailed through that one.'

`Yer've passed Inspectors' exam? Well fuck me drunk, I always knew yer'd make the grade Jacobs. There were always summat about you as set yer apart from rest. So, ave yer applied for an Inspectors' post then?'

`Well, thing is, I don't really want to leave area so I'm prepared to wait for summat to come up here, which it did a few months back. I thought I were in wi' a shout but then a DI transferred from up Newcastle an' that were that.'

`Bit o' tough shit that lad. What's he like then, this new DI?'

`Oh, he's a sound bloke, can be a bit moody at times but can't we all?'

`Aye, most of us any road lad. Can't say as I remember you ever being the moody sort though. No matter what sort o' shit we were dealing wi', yer were always there wi' that big smile o' yours an' ready to pass on one o' yer Mams' pearls o' wisdom. It's been bloody good seeing yer again D.J., we'll have to meet up for a pint or three sometime, ave a proper catch-up.'

`I'd like that Sir. Anyway, thanks for yer time an' for this.' Jacobs patted the box-file. `I'll leave yer to get back to yer bikes then, it's been great seeing you an' all Sir.'

Jacobs picked up the file and prepared to leave.

`Not so fast Sergeant! Where are yer going from here?'

`I'll be heading back to station an' get started on this little lot.'

`Perfect, another ten minutes won't hurt owt then. Wait there, I'll just go change mi shirt an' yer can gi' me a lift into town. Tuesday's market day an' I generally go for a couple o' pints on market day. Don't mind dropping me somewhere near Masons do yer?'

`It'd be my pleasure Sir.'

`Good, that's sorted then. Won't be a tick.'

Chapter 18

Wednesday 18th January, 10.30 a.m.

`It's just a thought D.J. but I've been thinking about those papers your old boss gave you yesterday and the thing is, it's going to be a very time-consuming process to search through that lot and I'm not quite sure how many man hours I can justify on raking through an old colleagues' memoirs. So, here's the thought, why don't I see if our old friend Logan Harvey would be prepared to give em the once-over, it strikes me that it could be right up his street.'

`I think it's a cracking idea Sir. I reckon he'd be a damn sight quicker than us as well an', if I'm honest, I weren't really looking forward to fighting mi way through that lot. Me an' paperwork aren't reyt compatible at the best o' times.'

`That's settled then. We'll swing by his place on our way back to the station later.'

The two detectives were just approaching the outskirts of Retford on their way to Rampton Secure Hospital and their appointment with Brian Suttons' case workers.

`Ave yer ever been down here before Troy?'

`No, this is a first for me D.J., what about you?'

`Just the once, must be about ten years back. I came to arrest a bloke as worked here, one o' orderlies he was. Any road, we'd been after this rapist who'd struck about half a dozen times around Donny but never left any traces behind. Apparently, he believed in safe rape an' always used a Johnny. Any road, that's how we finally caught him, you're gonna love this Troy. His last victim, after the deed was done so to speak, grabbed him by the bollocks and squeezed for all she was worth. Well o' course our man slaps her a couple o' times to make her let go, which of course she eventually did but not before she's managed to rip the Johnny off and scoop out a small amount of its contents, which she then smeared inside her, shall we say, recently violated area. Laddo pulls his pants up grabs the Johnny an' legs it an' she calmly walks into the nearest nick an' explains what's happened. We'd got his DNA on file from an earlier arrest for assault or summat an' Bill Quinn sent me an' a couple o' uniforms down here to bring him in. He got eighteen years but had only served three afore he were found in prison showers wi' his throat cut an' his cock in his mouth an' they say there's no justice eh?'

`What an incredible story.'

`She were an incredible woman Troy. One o' the female officers who dealt with her told me later that she were cool as a cucumber throughout the whole thing. Apparently, she said no woman should have to go through such an horrific ordeal an' she felt as if she'd struck a blow for women everywhere. When my colleague agreed she said `It's not just that love, his breath stank an' his B.O were terrible. No woman should have to lay under owt like that.'

`Unbelievable, imagine having the presence of mind to do what she did under such dreadful circumstances.'

`Aye. Reyt, looks like we're here, might take us a while to clear security though.'

Jacobs eased the car to a stop and cut the engine.

****

Rampton Secure Hospital lies between Retford and Rampton in the Bassetlaw district of Nottinghamshire, approximately one and a half miles from Rampton village. It is home to about four hundred patients, detained there under the Mental Health Act of nineteen-eighty-three. However, about a quarter of these have had no significant contact with the criminal justice system but have been detained owing to their `dangerous, violent, or criminal propensities'. The remainder have been convicted of an offence and been either ordered to be detained in hospital or subsequently transferred there from prison. Part of the criteria for admission requires that patients must present a `grave and immediate danger to the public and/or themselves.'

Some of it's more notable inmates have included `Angel of Death' Beverley Allitt, armed robber Charles Salvador aka Bronson, and Soham killer Ian Huntley, who was sectioned there for two months following his arrest after dribbling and refusing to speak. Psychiatrists later concluded that he was not mentally ill but had merely feigned madness in a forlorn attempt to evade justice for his crime.

These were the surroundings in which Dennis and Jacobs now found themselves, the formers patience now wearing thin.

`This is a fucking joke! Forty-five minutes we've been standing around here like a pair of spare pricks. For crying out loud our appointment was for eleven o'clock and it's now nearly half-past. We're officers of the law for fucks sake, not bastard inmates.' He seethed.

`We prefer to use the term patients, if you don't mind Sir.'

The two detectives turned to see a tall, bespectacled man in his early forties, who had silently entered the small waiting room.

`And I prefer not to be kept waiting around like some sort of jilted bride. Maybe a charge of wasting police time might go some way to curing you of your tardiness.'

`I can assure you Sir, my lateness in coming to meet you was neither intentional or avoidable. We had a bit of an incident earlier which, unfortunately, turned into an all hands on deck situation. I can only apologise. I'm Doctor Donnelly by the way, David Donnelly.'

`Detective Inspector Dennis, this is my colleague Sergeant Jacobs.' Dennis said, shaking the offered hand. `If we could perhaps get straight down to business, I know it's a well-worn phrase but we really are extremely busy.'

`As are we Inspector, however, I can only apologise again for keeping you waiting, if you'd like to come this way gentlemen.'

Doctor Donnelly led them down a short corridor to a large, comfortable-looking office.

`Right gentlemen...' He began, once he and Dennis were seated. Jacobs, as always, was standing a few feet away. `... I've been the psychiatrist in charge of Brian Suttons' case for the last fifteen years or so. My predecessor, James Bush, should be joining us shortly. In fact, I rather thought he would be here by now, I can't think what's keeping him.'

`Must be a trait of your profession.' Dennis grumbled, before adding, `Sorry Doctor, low blow that one.'

`Mmm, quite. Anyway, how may I be of assistance?'

Troy Dennis spent the next ten minutes familiarising Donnelly with the events of the last week.

`... so you see Doctor, even though we don't actually have a positive identification of the remains, the chances of them belonging to anybody else are, to say the least, remote. Ergo, the possibility that Brian Sutton did not kill Simon West becomes a distinct probability.'

` That really is very interesting Inspector. As I said earlier, Brian has been a patient of mine for about fifteen years. Before then Doctor Bush, who really should be here any time, was responsible for his case and, to be honest, he has always expressed reservations about his guilt...'

`More than just reservations David, there's no way Sutton did what he said and you bloody well know it.'

A loud, disembodied voice emanated around the room.

`What the f...' Jacobs blurted, looking all around him.

`Ha-ha, ha-ha. Sorry gentlemen, I really couldn't resist that. Ooh, the looks on your faces.'

A small man, no more than five feet tall, about seventy-years-old, revealed himself from his hiding-place behind one of the curtains that hung in the window at the opposite end of the room.

`I've been sitting on that windowsill since eleven o' clock this morning waiting for you buggers to show-up. Allow me to introduce myself, Jim Bush, one-time practitioner of the noble art of psychiatry at this hallowed establishment.'

`Really Jim, this is too much...'

`Oh, don't be such a boring fart David. You really need to lighten up a bit.'

`I must agree with Doctor Donnelly.' Dennis said now. `I'm not sure you appreciate the gravity of the situation, jumping out from behind the curtains like some modern-day Wizard of Oz.'

`On the contrary Inspector, I had the decency to arrive for our meeting in good time and I get bored rather easily these days. I had intended to just jump out on David and give him a shock when he came in but when the three of you entered together I couldn't resist indulging in a spot of eavesdropping. Now, shall we get down to business?'

`Unless you'd rather have another game of `Hide and Seek' or perhaps `Musical Chairs' even?' Dennis said bad-naturedly.

`Maybe later, if you're not too busy.' Bush laughed.

`Jim, please, I'm sure we've all got more important things to do.' Donnelly pleaded.

`You lot might have, I'm not so busy these days but alright then. My apologies Inspector. Believe it or not, I am actually capable of serious conversation, shall we?'

The little man perched himself on the edge of the coffee-table that separated Dennis and Donnelly. Jacobs, for his part, was valiantly fighting the urge to laugh out loud.

`You're of the opinion Doctor Bush that Brian Sutton did not murder Simon West?'

`Absolutely, Sutton topped his step-father, no doubt about that but he had nothing whatsoever to do with killing that young boy.'

`What makes you so sure and, if you don't mind me saying, why are we only learning of your doubts now?'

`Inspector, I have been expressing my doubts about Suttons' guilt from the very first time I met him as a young man more than thirty years ago. If I'd had my way that particular murder conviction would have been overturned soon after. However, I am but one voice.'

`You still haven't told us why you are so sure of his innocence.'

`His whole story is a figment of an imagination fuelled by a below average intelligence and a yearning for notoriety.'

`Jim, that's really not fair.' Donnelly said. `In recent years Brian has come on leaps and bounds. He now has an I.Q. in the region of...'

`Oh, give over with the bollocks David for Christs' sake. The man's well over fifty now and may well have learned something during his long incarceration but the facts are he was little more than a retard when he was first committed in eighty-three.'

`Jim! That's not the sort of language we use as you well...'

`And shove the politically correct shit where the sun don't shine as well.' Bush said angrily.

`Gentlemen, please, can we get back on track?' Dennis said. `You were saying Doctor Bush?'

`Call me Jim Inspector, I'm not one of those pretentious arseholes who insists on using my former title into retirement. As I was saying, Sutton killed his step-father and while in custody, for whatever reason, he invented a scenario where he killed the West boy as well. I heard everything you told David, from behind the curtain, the fact that the boy was beaten to death and not stabbed proves his whole story was nothing but fabrication.'

`But why were you so sure he was lying beforehand?'

`Brian Sutton never stood much of a chance in life Inspector. His father was killed when the boy was young and the mother took up with an abusive spouse. He was constantly ridiculed at school because of his long nose and scruffy appearance. This, combined with a below average intelligence, produced a very disturbed young man. Part of his confession concerns the sexual assault of the child in question. I believe the phrase he used was that he gave him `a damn good fucking'?'

Dennis nodded.

`I would have no hesitation in saying that this was impossible. You see Inspector, Brian Sutton was born with a condition known as micro penis, a rather severe form in his case I'm afraid. To put it bluntly Inspector, he is a fifty-three year old man sporting the wedding tackle of a toddler. This coupled with the fact that he is completely impotent makes me seriously doubt his ability to administer a fucking of any description let alone a damn good one. To fully answer your question, it is my belief that Sutton, whilst basking in the glory of his arrest for killing his step-father admitted to the other murder in an attempt to increase his importance and may well have admitted culpability in any other unsolved crimes had he known of them.'

`If, as you say, you've been raising these concerns for more than thirty years why was nothing ever done about his case?'

`Well, originally that would have been down to Henry Dutton. He was the top man here back then. I remember going to him on numerous occasions and voicing my concerns, all to no avail. In fact, old Henry was quite dismissive, almost contemptuous, in his refusal to give any credence to my ideas. On one occasion, he even threatened to have me removed from my post if I didn't `toe the line' as he put it.'

`I see. Well, thanks very much for your time Do... er, Jim. Would it be possible to see our man Sutton now Doctor Donnelly?'

`Of course Inspector. If you wouldn't mind waiting here for a few minutes, I'll go and get things sorted.'

`Yes, off you go David. Don't worry, I'll look after our two detective friends. We'll be down in the canteen when you've finished pissing about. Come on boys, follow me.'

****

`Let me apologise again for my behaviour back there gentlemen, I understand that my sense of humour is not to everybody's taste but I just can't help myself sometimes.' Jim Bush said a few minutes later.

`Forget it Jim, no harm done. If I wasn't so wound up with all the waiting about this morning, I may well have seen the funny side myself.' Dennis waved his hand in the air dismissively and took a drink from his coffee cup. `Christ, that's disgusting.' He grimaced.

`What mi Mam calls witches piss.' Jacobs agreed, placing his own hardly touched drink well out of arms reach.

`Observe, one of the benefits of being both retired and off duty.'

Bush produced a hip flask and proceeded to lace his own cup with a generous measure of its contents.

`Quite possibly an injustice to a perfectly good brandy but at least mine's drinkable.' He smiled.

`Pardon me for asking Sir but did I detect a certain animosity between yourself and Doctor Donnelly a few minutes back?' Jacobs asked now.

`That might be putting it a bit strongly Sergeant but you're right, David and I don't see eye to eye on a lot of things. He sees me as a bit of a dinosaur and I think he's a stuck-up, pretentious prick.'

`Care to elaborate?' asked Dennis.

`Call it a generational clash if you like. The thing is, I remember David first starting here, recently qualified and full of modern ideas, ready to change the world for the better. By that time, I had been working in this field for almost thirty years, either here or at Broadmoor. Then, all of a sudden, my methods were being called into question on a regular basis, the new brooms were sweeping clean, the old guard like myself were being either blatantly ignored or gradually put out to pasture.'

`Are yer sure it's not just a case of professional jealousy?' Jacobs asked, not unkindly.

`Trust me Sergeant, I have many vices but jealousy is certainly not one of them.' Bush laughed. `No, let me try and explain. As I said earlier, I have spent many years plying my trade, so to speak. From an early age, I've had a fascination with the criminal mind and its workings and to that end I have dedicated my whole adult life to its study. Now for the controversial bit. I, unlike many of my contemporaries, do not believe that these people can be cured. The best we can hope for, in my opinion, is that we may be able to understand and at the same time help they themselves to understand, what it is that drove them to do things they did.'

`Fascinating.' Dennis said. `So, I assume that Doctor Donnelly is of a different opinion and believes that all these patients can be cured?'

`Well, you would have to ask him that Inspector. Suffice it to say, he feels a certain, I don't know, empathy with his subjects that I never did. To be brutally honest, most of the men and women I've treated have been lacking in any attributes worthy of sympathy. In many cases they were little more than vicious animals.'

`Sounds a bit harsh, if yer don't mind me saying Sir.' Jacobs said.

`And that, in a nutshell Sergeant, is why I found my methods and opinions increasingly frowned upon. Just out of curiosity Sergeant, if a Rottweiler or Pit Bull Terrier was to attack and kill a young child, would you think that by placing the dog into a different, perhaps more loving, environment that one day that dog might be deemed safe around children?'

`Of course not. Look, I know where yer going wi' this but...'

`I'm not sure you do Sergeant, I wasn't trying to trick you into anything. Of course, the dog should be put down, it's beyond rehabilitation and the chance of it doing the same again is too great to risk. Now, I'm not saying we should necessarily treat a man who rapes and murders a child in the same way we would a dog, although many people do feel that way. No, my point is, how in Gods' name can we possibly think that a bit of therapy and tender loving care will cure a man of the urge to commit such a heinous crime again? As I said earlier, I've spent a life time studying these people but my reasons have been purely to try and understand the whys and wherefores, not because of some poxy moral crusade.'

`But surely you've found extenuating circumstances in many cases?' Dennis asked.

`Like abusive parents or broken homes perhaps? You'd be surprised Inspector, or perhaps in your line of work you wouldn't, just how many of the most violent and twisted people come from a good solid background. I myself was sexually abused from the ages of four to seven by a friend of my fathers but as far as I know I've lived a law-abiding life and have certainly never felt the need to abuse another.

Do you see now why I feel almost like a pariah? I know more about the workings of the criminal mind than anyone I've ever met but my inability to empathise sets me apart.'

`It's certainly been a very enlightening conversation.' Dennis said.

`One more thing Inspector before David gets here.'

`Yes?'

`Sutton's a particularly odious sort of character, absolutely no saving graces that I'm aware of but to the best of my knowledge it's many years since he's had any contact with the police.'

`And?'

`Well, I think if you can somehow manage to push the right buttons, so to speak, you might just get what you came here for. Right, David will be here soon to take you to your meeting. Been a pleasure lads, maybe we'll meet again sometime.'

The little man jumped up from his chair, shook hands with the two detectives, and almost skipped out of the canteen.

`Well, what do you make of that D.J.?'

`To be honest Sir, I'm not sure if he's off home or back to one o' cells in here. Dunt seem reyt caring for a doctor, does he?'

`What do you think he meant about pushing the right buttons with Sutton?'

`Dunno Sir but I'm sure we'll work summat out. Any road, look sharp, here comes the doc.'

****

A few moments later, in an interview room that was almost like a suite at the Hilton Hotel compared with the surroundings the two policemen were accustomed to, Troy Dennis was sitting across a table from the man he had come here to see. Doctor Donnelley was reclining on a small sofa a few feet away while Jacobs, as was his custom, was standing just inside the door.

The years had not been good to Brian Sutton. Although he was only fifty-three, one could be forgiven for thinking him closer to seventy. His face was deeply lined and only a few tufts of wispy, grey, hair clung in patches to his head. When he had smiled at Jacobs upon being introduced only three, well-spaced and deeply nicotine-stained teeth had been visible. All this, combined with his long, pointed nose, bulging-eyes, and almost deathly pallor resulted in an almost frightening visage.

My God, it's every child's nightmare, thought Dennis

Fuck me, yer were an ugly bastard at school but yer've taken it to a whole new level now Pongo, Jacobs thought.

`I assume you know why we're here Brian?'

`Aye, yer want to know about that little bastard as I killed years back.'

His voice was little more than a whisper, adding to the sense of menace his appearance provoked.

`That's right Brian. Now, I wonder if you could take us through exactly what you remember about that day.'

`I'll tell yer same as I told them coppers years back an' same as I've been telling these bastards in here ever since. I'll never tell anybody where to find him. All as I'll say is, I fucked the arse off the little twat, then I slit his throat an' stabbed him til' I'd had mi fill. He squealed like a stuck pig I can tell yer.' At this Sutton broke out into a rasping laugh that ended in a fit of coughing.

`Yes. Well you see, that's where we have a slight problem Brian. The thing is, we've found young Simon Wests' body and I'm afraid that a big part of your story just doesn't ring true.'

`What part? Your coppers are all the bastard same, yer just trying to trick me.'

`Not at all Brian, no tricks I assure you.'

`Then what the hell yer going on about?'

`Simon wasn't stabbed Brian. So, you're either mistaken or lying. Which one is it Brian?'

`No! you're the one that's fuckin lying copper. I'm telling yer I slit the little bastards' throat an' stabbed him but before I done that I gave him a right good f...'

`Fuck this! I've heard enough of this bollocks...'

In three quick paces Dean Jacobs covered the short distance from the door and planted his large hands firmly on the table.

`Now, you listen to me Pongo yer snivelling little bastard. Yer never went near that young lad an' we all know it. As for all this shite about sexually assaulting him yer'd be hard pressed to knock out a wank wi that tiny thing you've got. In fact, I bet yer can't even go for a slash wi'out yer piss on at least three fingers. So, you take my advice an' start answering the Inspectors' questions honestly or, God help me, the doc over there'll be finding me a room here for the foreseeable after I've done wi yer.'

The result of this uncharacteristic outburst was both immediate and astounding. Doctor Donnelley jumped to his feet ready to remonstrate with Jacobs for what he saw as little short of police brutality, Dennis made to get out of his chair in an effort to placate the psychiatrist, Jacobs himself seemed to come to his senses. All, however, were stopped in their tracks by the reaction of Brian Sutton.

He collapsed forward onto the table with his head held in his hands.

`It's true, it's all true.' He wailed loudly. `I never touched him, I don't know what happened to the little bastard. All I did was burn his stuff so you lot wunt find it.'

He looked up with tears streaming down his face. His eyes, if it were at all possible, seemed to be bulging even further from his head. All in all, rather than looking menacing, Brian Sutton now cut a pathetic figure.

`Gentlemen.' Donnelley said now. `I think it's time we called a halt to these proceedings. I don't think I have ever been party to such a blatant abuse of authority and you can rest assured that I will be taking this matter fur...'

`Leave it doc. I'm alright.' Sutton wiped his nose with the back of a filthy, nicotine-stained fingered hand. `It's about time as the truth were told.'

`Brian, I really don't think...'

`I cunt give a fuck what yer think. Thirty-odd bastard years I've been listening to you lot spouting yer shit. Well time's come, I've had enough. Ask thi questions Inspector, I'm ready to answer em.'

Sutton had quite suddenly undergone another startling transformation. Gone was the blubbering wreck of a few moments previously, in its place was a cool, calm figure. The sinister whisper had also been replaced by an easier to discern timbre.

`Right, well, err... what exactly did you mean when you said you'd burned his stuff?' Dennis asked now.

`The day I killed that bastard Blake, I took whatever money he'd got an' went darn to off-licence for some cans an' fags. Well, I knew I cunt go back home so, I pissed off o'er Minneymoor for a drink an' a smoke to celebrate. Any road, while I were there I found some shorts an' a t-shirt all covered in blood. Well, I recognised shirt as belonging to lad as disappeared a few days afore cos he'd been wearing it one day when him an' his mates had been giving me grief. So, I had mesen a little fire an' burnt the lot so as you lot wunt get yer hands on em.'

`Why on earth would you do something like that?' Dennis asked.

`Why not? It were bad enough getting hassle off folk mi own age an' bastard Blake wi'out having to put up wi' it off o' young uns an' all.'

`But why not just leave it at that? Why admit to a crime you didn't commit?'

`I did it just for laugh at first but then your lot started believing me so I carried it on. I allus thought as police would find him eventually an' catch the bloke as really did it but yer never did.'

`And thanks to you we may never do. Good Christ man! Have you any idea the problems you've caused?'

`Guess what Inspector?... I cunt give a fuck.' Sutton smiled nastily.

`Obviously not. Where exactly did you find these blood-stained clothes?'

`If yer cut down path that leads onto field from top o' Donny Road just off to yer reyt there's a rock as looks a bit like a table that's slanting a bit. They were tucked into a space just underneath that, all rolled-up like. I burnt em on rock had another drink an' forgot all about em till your lot got me for Blake.'

`So why come clean now, after all this time?'

Sutton shrugged his shoulders.

`Why not? By sounds of it you lot, especially that fat bastard over there...' He jerked his head towards Jacobs who had retaken his customary position by the door. `... dint believe I'd killed him anyway, not like that soft twat on sofa.'

`Well, I think we're all done here. Thank you for your help, grudging as it was. We'll see ourselves out Doctor.'

`Oy! Fat Man.' Sutton suddenly said. `If I ever get out of here I'm gonna come looking for you an' yer'll get what that bastard Blake got.'

`I'll look forward to it Pongo but I'd best not hold mi breath eh?' Jacobs winked and followed Dennis out of the door.

****

`Well, I've got to say that was a bit of a turn-up for the books D.J. I always thought that if we ever got the chance to play good-cop/bad-cop that the roles would be reversed.'

`Aye, I'm sorry about that Troy. Don't know what came over me, I just lost it for a couple o' minutes.'

The two men were walking across the hospital car-park to where they had left their vehicle.

`Bollocks to sorry man, at least we now know beyond any doubt that Sutton wasn't responsible for young Wests' murder. Admittedly, we're no closer to finding the real culprit but at least now we've one less blind alley up which to lose ourselves.'

`I'm not so sure about that Troy. Did yer see him back there, it were almost as if he were three different people. I mean, which Pongo do we believe?'

`Oh, I'm not saying we take every word he said as Gospel by any means but I'm reasonably sure that his reaction to your taunting, for want of a better description, of him couldn't possibly have been faked. No, I'm with Jim Bush on this one. There's absolutely no way that our man in there killed Simon West. All that remains for us now is to find who did and that my friend, may well be easier said than done. One other thing D.J., just how well do you actually know Sutton, what was all that Pongo bollocks?'

`He were three or four years above me at school. I never really *knew* him as such but all the kids knew who Pongo was. He got that nickname after a character in one o' kids comics at time. `Pongo Snodgrass' were a scruffy, ugly, little fucker wi' a long, pointy nose. Yer must admit, it suits him down to ground.'

`Yes well, I think old Pongo in there has taken up quite enough of our time and energy. We've g...'

`Ay up Denno, D.J., fancy bumping into you two here.'

Logan Harvey was walking across the car-park towards them.

`Alreyt Loge mate, how's it going?'

`Not too bad D.J., Yerself?'

`Can't grumble pal.' Jacobs said, shaking him warmly by the hand.

`What on earth brings you here?' Dennis asked, offering his own hand.

`Would you believe I'm doing a bit of research for a new book?'

`I thought South Yorkshire history was your field, what could possibly interest you in a place like this?'

`Well... it's a bit embarrassing really...'

`Come on Logan, we're all friends here there's no need to be shy, is there D.J.?'

`None whatsoever Troy.' Jacobs smiled.

`Well, yer gonna find out sooner or later I suppose. I'm here to see Terry Williams.'

`Yer kidding! What the fuck do yer want wi' him?' Jacobs asked incredulously.

Terry Williams and his partner in crime, Ernie Butler, were the two men responsible for the `Blackleg' murders of a couple of months previously. Logans' father, Ronnie, had been their first victim although it had later come to light that their killing spree had actually started many years earlier.

`I know how it must look but, the thing is, he got in touch wi' me a few days back asking if I'd be interested in writing, I suppose you could call it his biography, a warts an' all account of his life and deeds.'

`Are you sure it's really a good idea?' asked Dennis. `I mean, I'm pretty sure there's rules about criminals benefiting financially in any way from their crimes.'

`That's the thing yer see Denno, he's stated quite categorically that any proceeds to which he might be entitled be shared equally by the surviving families of his victims and various homeless charities.'

`That's allus assuming anybody wants to read it in first place.' Jacobs put in.

`Yer'd be surprised D.J., this sort o' stuff sells like hot cakes. Yer should see some o' the shit Niamh likes to read, her `abuse books' I call em, owt that deals wi other folks' misery, so long as it's true, an' she laps it up. Her sister's as bad.'

`Well, I suppose there's nowt so queer as folk, as mi old Mam likes to say.'

`As it happens Logan, you've just saved us a wasted journey. We were on our way to see you from here. There's a few documents I'd like you to have a look at, if you can spare the time of course, what with this new project you've got yourself?'

`No worries Denno, I can always spare the time to try an' help. What sort o' documents are we talking about?'

Dennis spent the next five minutes giving Logan a quick run-down on what he wanted.

`Sounds intriguing, drop em off whenever mate an' I'll give em a good looking over for yer. Reyt, I'd best be getting off then. Are yer going up for quiz at Hill Top later?'

`I doubt it but you never know. I'll get those papers to you as soon as though.'

The three friends bade their farewells and went their separate ways. Logan in search of a known murderer, Dennis and Jacobs on a quest to unearth one.

Chapter 19

Thursday 19th January 2017

`I'm sick of this shit!'

The tall, slightly stooped figure angrily pushed his plate across the table.

`Beans on toast, spaghetti on toast, beans and *sausage* on toast. How long have we been eating this crap for now lads? A week? Ten days? Longer? Where's that doddering old bastard got to anyway? He's not usually away this long. I'll see you in a few days he said, there's plenty of food and drink to see you by until then he said. Well lads, I've got news for yer, that was the last of the wine.' He drained his glass before slamming it violently onto the table. `All as we've got left now is about a dozen cans o' lager an' a couple o' bottles o' cheap cider. Food wise we're down to a loaf or two o' bread two blocks o' cheese an' a couple o' cans o' tuna. How long's that gonna last eh?'

His three companions just stared mutely back at him from their respective positions at the table.

`What, nothing to say for yourselves? Porthos? Athos? Not even you Aramis? Oh, I see, let's just leave it to d'Artagnan to drag us out o' the shit again is it? Some fuckin musketeers you three turned out to be. Right, well let me tell yer what's going to happen then. That old bastard's got until tomorrow afternoon to get his arse down here wi' some proper snap or I'm going walkabouts again an' fuck the rules! Ah, got your attention now lads ant I? Well, one of us as got to do summat ant they. Right, that's settled then, one for all an' all for one eh lads?'

His three companions all smiled back at him

`That's the spirit lads, that's the spirit.'

Chapter 20

Thursday 19th January 2017, 11.00 a.m.

CID H.Q., Doncaster.

Dennis and Jacobs were gathered in the formers' small office, each with a bacon sandwich from the police canteen and a mug of coffee, courtesy of Dennis' machine.

`Why do we do it to ourselves D.J.?' Dennis asked suddenly.

`What's that then Troy?'

`This.' He held his half-eaten breadcake before him. `I've a good mind to arrest the whole catering staff under the trades descriptions act. If that's really bacon I'll show my arse on the Keepmoat pitch the next time Donny are at home. If that came off a pig it must have been a bloody anorexic one.'

`Mebbe it were a guinea pig.' Laughed Jacobs. `But... if yer don't want it...' he said holding out his hand expectantly.

`No, no. I'll force myself. After all, we don't know when we'll get another chance to eat. What do you think are our chances of getting your Mother to take over the running of the canteen? At least we'd be assured of edible fare then.'

`Aye, yer reyt there. Mind yer, I don't think Health an' Hygiene would be too happy wi' her having a fag burning in ashtray beside her while she were frying bacon.'

`Probably not, more's the pity.'

Just then there was a sharp knock on the door and Andy Gibbons walked in.

`Thought yer'd like to know straight away Boss. We've managed to trace Anthony West, or Tony North as he's known now. He changed his name by deed-poll years ago, about the time he moved down Cornwall.'

`Very imaginative, from West to North. Go on Andy.'

`It seems he went off o' rails a bit as a youth an' then about twenty years or so back straightened himself out, changed his name an' moved to Cornwall. Lives the life of a surfer-boy from what I can make out.'

`And do police appeals and news reports not make it as far as St. Ives or wherever?'

`He's just returned from Australia Boss, where he's been `chasing the waves' as he put it for the past month. He only found out we were looking for him late last night, called us as soon as he managed to `drag myself out of bed' as he put it. Any road, he's got a few business matters to sort out down there an' he'll be with us late morning tomorrow.'

`Okay, thanks Andy.'

`One other thing Boss. He asked me if it would be alright for him to see the body, I told him I dint think it'd be a problem, hope that's okay?'

`That's fine Andy. However, it's more skeletal remains than a body, there's not really anything left of the brother he remembers.'

`He's fully aware of that Sir, reckons it might help give him a bit of closure after all these years.'

`Okay, thanks again Andy.'

`No probs Boss.'

Gibbons left, closing the door gently behind him.

`Well, that's all well and good. We should have a positive i.d. within the next couple of days but we're still no nearer to discovering the real perpetrator. Any fresh ideas D.J.?'

`Nowt as jumps straight to mind, no. Wi' a bit o' luck Logan might be able to dredge summat up from them old papers as Bill Quinn gave us.'

`Mmm, possibly but I think it's a long shot at best. There's got to be something we're missing man. To be honest D.J., I'm not sure how much longer we can justify spending so many man hours on a thirty-five-year old case.'

`Well, as much as it pains me to say it Troy, the only thing as I can suggest is hitting the records again, going through all old files an' checking any similar disappearances from round same time.'

`I know what you're saying, the thought hardly fills my heart with joy either. Tell you what D.J., you take the files twenty years before young West disappeared and I'll take from then to the present day. We'll have the rest of the day trawling through those, see if we can't turn anything up. Meet back here at, oh... five-thirty and we'll compare notes over a pint or three.'

`Right yer are Troy, sounds like a plan. Chin up mate, summat'll turn up sooner or later, I can feel it in mi water.'

`Yes, well let's just hope that doesn't turn out to be some unfortunate urinary infection. Five-thirty then D.J.'

The big Sergeant tugged at his forelock and left the room, closing the door gently behind him.

Chapter 21

1.30 p.m.

`Grandad, we're here! Grandad? Nannan, where's Grandad?'

Two-years-old Maisie asked Niamh Harvey, a look akin to panic appearing on her face.

`He must be in the kitchen silly.'

Molly, her twin sister, said matter-of-factly before charging through towards the kitchen, hastily shedding her coat as she went.

`Nannan, he's not in here as well. Where's our Grandad?' she demanded.

This wasn't right, if Grandad wasn't sat in his corner of the sofa, watching the telly, then he was *always* at the kitchen table making his books.

`I don't know girls, maybe he's just gone to the shop or something, I'm sure he won't be long.'

`But it's thirsty Nannan an' Grandad knows we always come on thirsty for chippies.' Maisie said now.

`Yes and we've bringed him some blasted sausages and some curly sauce from the fishing and chippies shop.' Her sister agreed.

`Don't worry girls, we all know Grandad won't miss his battered sausages, they're his favourite. He'll be here in a minute, bet yer any money. Now, shall we get the plates and knives and forks ready?'

`Okay Nannan but he better get here before they go cold cos he still has to eat them, doesn't he?'

`Yes Maisie, we don't like waste in this h...'

`Is that battered sausage I smell? And curry sauce from the chippy as well? And... and... GRAND-DAUGHTERS!'

A loud, menacing, voice could be heard to the accompaniment of heavy footsteps coming down the stairs.

The two girls looked at each other with a combination of fear and glee on their faces, before diving as one underneath the kitchen table where they remained, valiantly trying to stifle their giggles, as Logan Harvey entered the room.

`Well that's strange, I'm sure I could smell Em an' Em a minute ago.' He said now, scratching his head theatrically.

`I don't think so Grandad, I haven't seen them all day.' Niamh played along.

`But it's Thursday, they always come to see me on Thursday. Oh well, I might get my sausages in peace today, are they nearly ready?'

`Yes. Why don't you sit down at the table and I'll fetch them over?'

`What a good idea.' He said, pulling out a chair.

`HA, HA, we tricked you!' the two girls squealed in unison as they erupted from their hiding place each hugging one of his legs and vying for his attentions.

`Come here you pair o' monkeys.' He laughed reaching down and easily picking one up in each arm. `Yer frightened yer old Grandad half to death.'

`You're rubbish at hide and sleep Grandad, you never find us' Maisie giggled.

`Cos we're the bestest at hiding in this house.' Her sister joined in.

`Ah, but I've got you both now.' He laughed, swinging them both round to another chorus of giggles.

`Come on everybody, dinner's ready. Let's eat it all up while it's still hot.' Niamh said now.

`And then we can watch `Paw Patrol' with Grandad.' Maisie said.

`And `Ben and Holly.' Molly joined in.

`Only if everybody eats all their dinner.' Logan warned.

`It's a deal!' the twins screamed in unison.

****

Two hours later, with the twins safely back under their mothers' jurisdiction, Logan and Niamh sat smoking at their kitchen table.

`So what was so top secret earlier that yer felt the need to work upstairs rather than yer usual spot here?' Niamh asked.

`Who says I was working? Mebbe I just went for a lie-down.'

`Try again mister, or are you forgetting that I know you better than yer know yerself? Is it this new Williams book that's bothering you, yer've been a bit quiet since yer went to see him yesterday?'

`Have I? I've not meant to be.'

`Well, maybe quiet's the wrong way to describe it, I probably mean more, deep in thought like. Listen Logan, if it's gonna be too much for you, yer can tell Terry Williams to shove his memoirs as far up his arse as he can get em. After what he did yer don't owe him fuck all.'

`I know that love but I've got to admit it's really got mi juices flowing and the fact that he won't benefit from it financially eases mi conscience a bit. Any road, that's not what I were busy wi earlier. I were going through some old papers Denno asked me to have a look at.'

`Oh yeah? An' when did yer see him like?'

`Yesterday when I went to see Williams, he were at Rampton on police business. I told yer last night.'

`No Logan, yer dint. See? That's what I mean. Once yer get yer teeth into summat yer seem to go into a world o' yer own, there's only Em an' Em as can get more than a couple o' words out o' yer when yer like that.'

Logan got up and moved round to the other side of the table, putting his arms round his wife.

`I hope you're not trying to accuse me of neglecting you.' He said, squeezing her and nuzzling her neck. `Cos we've got the house ourselves now yer know, I could show yer my appreciation.'

`Get off me, yer dunt know where I've been.' She laughed. `An' yer need a shave before there'll be any o' *that*. Now, get back to yer own side o' table an' tell me about these papers o' Dennos.'

`I remember the days when yer cunt keep yer hands off me.' He said, pretending to sulk and returning to his chair.

`An' I remember the days when yer always shaved before coming to see me, even if yer were stinking of yer Grandads' Old Spice.'

`You always said yer liked Old Spice.'

`Yeah, when mi Dad wore it. Now stop changing subject an' tell me about these papers.'

`Suit yerself mardy arse, your loss. Can yer remember years ago when that Simon West disappeared?'

`Course I can, I think he were same year as our Pete. They reckon it's his body they found down on Minneymoor other week, don't they?'

`Well, it ant been confirmed yet but I don't think there's much doubt. Any road, the bloke as they've had locked up for it all these years apparently couldn't have done it an' Denno an' D.J. are stuck with a decades old murder investigation as a result.'

`So what're these papers then?'

`That's the interesting bit. It seems that the bloke as were in charge o' the original investigation never believed they'd got the right man in first place an' after his wife died he started digging around on his own trying to right a wrong. He kept a record of everything an' when he died these papers found their way to his old Sergeant, who just happens to be D.J.'s old gaffer. Denno an' D.J. have now passed em on to me.'

`Sounds complicated if yer ask me.'

`There's tons o' the bastard love, I've only flicked through a few pages as yet but some of it makes really interesting reading.'

`Well you'll have plenty to occupy your mind while I'm gone then.'

`Eh?'

`I'm off to York for the weekend, remember?'

`I'd forgot all about that. Well don't worry about me struggling through reams of old papers while you're off on the piss will yer?'

`Don't worry I won't. Anyway, why don't yer go upstairs an' run me a bath while yer having a shave? Then when yer all nice an' smooth yer can join me if yer like.'

Logan nearly knocked his chair over in his haste to reach the stairs, leaving Niamh laughing to herself at the table.

`Yer've still got it girl, got him right where yer want him.' She said quietly as she lit herself another cigarette.

Chapter 22

Excerpts from the papers of Cedric Short.

18th June 1994, 11.30.p.m.

Well my love, today we finally said our good byes just a few short months before our fifty-eighth wedding anniversary. I must admit lass that I'm feeling more than a little pissed-off with you at the moment, I thought we'd agreed all those years ago that I would be the one to go first, on account of me not being able to look after mesen without your help!

Just kidding Naomi love. What a way to go though girl, on the golf course on a beautiful summers day. It's only a pity we didn't get to finish our round, you really were playing beautifully, right up until you stumbled and fell as you were lining up your putt on the seventeenth. A massive brain haemorrhage the doctor told me, you wouldn't have known a thing about it, thank God.

Anyway love, the last of the mourners left this little cottage of ours a couple of hours ago (what a turn-out you got girl!) and I've decided that the Cotswolds without you would be nothing short of unbearable so, I'm selling-up and we're going home. I'll decide where to spread your ashes once we're back in good old Yorkshire or maybe I'll wait until my urn joins yours and the boys can decide. The eighteenth green at Town Moor perhaps? Fitting, don't you think?

For nigh on sixty years you've been my rock girl. I often thought of young Bill Quinn as being the Watson to my Holmes and he so often was. If that were true however, then every Sherlock needs a Mycroft to turn to when things get too much. That, my love, is a role you fulfilled with the greatest ability. Therefore, it will come as no surprise to you to learn that I am planning on taking my own `Last Bow'. I'm sure you know, without being told, to what I refer. I know I promised to leave coppering behind all those years back, and I did but now that you're no longer with me I fear I need something with which to occupy this old mind of mine. I aim to right a wrong Naomi love afore me an' thee meet again, wherever that might be. I know you'll understand, sleep tight sweetheart. Xx.

19th July 1996

Fourteen years to the day since anybody last saw hide or hair of young Simon West. If the powers that be are to be believed his murderer has been locked-up for most of that time. Absolute bollocks! There is no way on Gods' Earth that half-wit was responsible and I will not rest until I prove it.

4th February 1997

My God, it pains me to think of this murderer still walking free among us! Why would nobody listen to me at the time? Nearly forty years a copper and my opinions counted for nothing. Well I'll show em all, mark my words I will!

11th March 1998

I had a couple of drinks with young Bill Quinn today, *Detective Superintendent Bill Quinn,* no less! I always knew that boy would go far. Anyway, I ran some of my theories by him and he's assured me that he's going to look into them and get back to me. We're meeting again next week.

22nd March 1998

Apparently, some things never change, saw Bill Quinn again today and it seems that his superiors are as dismissive of my opinions as the likes of Ed Baker and his ilk were just before I retired. Theories are no use without evidence they say. That's all well and good but how am I supposed to gather the evidence without the power my badge once allowed me? Not to worry, the fight goes on.

27th December 1999

A new millennium fast approaches and still my erstwhile colleagues seem loath to act on my findings. Bill Quinn, God bless him, still shows faith in me and that helps keep the old spirits up. I feel sure that the break I'm looking for lurks just around the corner but which corner? That is the question.

28th July 2003

Alas, I fear that even young Bill Quinn has lost faith in his mentor. Oh, the lad's far too polite to say as much but I can't shake the feeling that he merely humours, nay almost pities, me at our meetings these days. Still, I do look forward to our, all too infrequent, little get-togethers. It seems Bill has also developed a taste for decent single-malt these days. The same can't be said for his smoking habits, he insists on smoking those vile miniature cigars. `Never did master the art of pipe-smoking Boss' he informed me recently. Twenty-one years since I was his boss and I still can't get him to call me Cedric, says he doesn't feel comfortable, the dozy bugger!

7th August 2006

What a bloody fool I made of myself earlier today! One of my great-granddaughters' university friends came round to interview me for some project or other she's doing about the changing face of law enforcement through the years or something like that. All I had to do was regale her with some of my old stories as Sophie had asked me to do. What did this silly old bastard do instead? I used the opportunity to try and get some support for my one-man-campaign for truth and justice, probably frightened the poor girl half to death. I wonder if flowers and chocolates are still acceptable as a form of apology to a young girl, like they were in my day. I'll ask Sophie tomorrow, better get some for her as well I suppose. Perhaps it's time I gave up on this crusade of mine, even Holmes himself was enjoying his retirement at eighty-nine, if he lived that long of course. I must remember to look that up.

17th February 2007

Six months if I'm lucky, that's how long the doctor's given me. If I can make it to the end of July I'll have managed ninety years on this mortal coil. It's almost thirteen years since you left me Naomi and I fear I've wasted every one of them. I am no closer now to proving that I put the wrong man away than I was on the day you died. I'm meeting young Bill again next week and I might just have one last go at convincing him but I don't hold out much hope.

That bastard at Rampton knows more than he's letting on, I'm sure of it. I'm sure he and Ed Baker were in cahoots somehow but Ed's long gone and, if the doctors are right, I won't be long in joining him so, I suppose I'll never know. Oh, curse this old age! Perhaps, one day the truth will finally come to light and, if that day comes, I hope there'll be someone still alive who remembers me. Old Cedric Short, they'll say, he were a stubborn, grumpy, old bastard but by Christ he were right all those years!

Chapter 23

Friday 20th January 2017, 11.40 a.m.

Logan Harvey sat back in his chair, removed his glasses, and rubbed the bridge of his nose tiredly. Niamh had stayed at her parents' house last night in preparation for the girls' weekend away in York, giving Logan the green light to do pretty much whatever he wanted for the next couple of days. However, five or six pints with Pete and Jud last evening had seen him making his way home for an early night but upon his return the lure of the papers that Denno had entrusted into his care had proved to be too much for his natural curiosity to bear. It had been almost three a.m. when he had finally dragged his weary body to bed. He had risen again at seven and, apart from the occasional toilet break, numerous cups of coffee, and even more cigarettes, those papers had held his undivided attention ever since. He lit another cigarette and thought over all he had read. There was absolutely no doubt in his mind that these were the writings of a highly intelligent individual. Such a damned shame, he thought now, that a man who had proved himself time and again to be without equal in his chosen profession had seen it necessary to dedicate so much of his well-deserved retirement to a crusade that everybody else seemed to have little, if any, interest in. Some of his diary entries, towards the end, painted the picture of an almost tortured soul.

Of everything Logan had read there was one piece that he kept coming back to. It was the closing sentences of a long letter which Cedric had written shortly before his death to his friend and former colleague Bill Quinn.

`... and so I urge you Young Bill to not just dismiss this as the ramblings of a bitter old man. I tell you, that bastard at Rampton and Ed Baker were thick as thieves, there's been a cover-up on a monumental scale. While we're at it, watch your back where that upstart Eric Dalton's

concerned as well, he's poison that one. He's also Ed Bakers' son-in-law, so he might well have something to do with all this.

Anyway, old friend this missive was supposed to be my way of saying goodbye just in case we two never meet again. I don't think I ever told you but you were always so much more than just a work colleague to me lad. I always used to say to Naomi that you were the trusted Watson to my Holmes. Do you know what she used to say? ` Don't be ridiculous Cedric, you know you think of him as a third son.' Happen we were both right lad eh?

On that point lad, I'd just like to say that I consider it an honour to have known and worked with you and to thank you for being there as a friend these last years.

To that end I hereby bequeath to you all my personal papers, some of them describe cases that you and I worked on together, others cases I worked whilst you were but a babe in arms. One day they might make interesting reading for somebody. In addition, I also leave you my copy of the complete collection of Sherlock Holmes stories, yes lad, the same one you so graciously sent to me upon my retirement all those years ago. I'm afraid the accompanying collection of single-malts are long-gone however!

Take care Young Bill, until we meet again.

Yours, Cedric (Boss to you!).

As in one of his later diary entries, the conclusion of this letter seemed to suggest that Cedric Short was convinced that the late Chief Constable Edward Baker and convicted murderer Brian Sutton had entered into some kind of conspiracy. Could this really be the case? Logan didn't think so but what right did he have to so easily dismiss the theories of a highly respected detective? And why had the spectre of Eric Dalton, so much a part of Logans' recent life, suddenly reared its ugly head again

He lit another cigarette. Yer gonna have to lay off these a bit an' all, he thought, that's twenty yer've gone through since yer came in last night for fucks' sake. He still couldn't quite shake the feeling that something in those last few lines could be important but he'd be damned if he knew what, or how.

An idea suddenly came to him and he reached for his mobile.

`Ay up Denno, it's Loge.'

`Yes I know mate, you don't have to be a detective to be able to read a phone screen yer know?'

`Alreyt smart arse but any detective worth his salt wouldn't have to keep relying on the services of an old pipe-fitter, would he?'

`Ooh, touchy! What can I do for you mate?'

`I was just wondering if there'd be any chance of me maybe meeting up with this Bill Quinn feller?'

`Logan, if you're onto something I want to know, we're banging our heads against the wall here at the minute.'

`It could be owt or nowt Denno. I've finished going through those papers you gave me, some of it's really interesting reading and would probably make a good book someday. Any road, there's one or two things that I've found a bit confusing an' I just thought mebbe if I could talk to somebody as actually knew him it might just shed a bit o' light on some of it. Oh, an' Eric Dalton's had a mention an' all.'

`What the fuck has he got to do with any of this?'

`Dunno pal, old Cedric had him down as a wrong un though. So, are yer gonna put me in touch wi' Bill Quinn or not?'

`I'll get D.J. to set a meeting up for you but Logan?'

`What?'

`You tell me the second you get anything you think could be useful.'

`O' course Denno, that goes wi' out saying mate.'

`Ok, I'll be in touch. I've got to go mate, I've got young Simon Wests' brother coming to see me anytime now.'

Logan placed his phone back on the table sighing. He hoped it wouldn't be too long before Denno got back in touch. Mebbe I should o' been a copper mesen, he thought, I hate having questions an' no answers.

Chapter 24

The tall, slightly stooped man gently replaced the grating on the large air-vent on the wall, taking great care to make as little noise as possible. In recent years, it hadn't been quite as easy for him to squeeze his frame through the tight opening. However, needs must and all that and none of the other three had showed any inclination to remedy the situation they had found themselves in so, as bastard usual, it fell to him to try and do something about it. He stood stock still for a few moments, dusting himself down, sniffing the air and making doubly sure that no-one was aware of his presence, before setting off and making his way to the main part of the house.

As always, the key to the back door could be found secreted underneath a large, stone Buddha that stood sentry just to the right of the door step. As he inserted the key into the lock however, he came to an abrupt halt.

Just what the fuck was that loud buzzing noise coming from the other side of the door? What's the silly old bastard been up to now?

Shrugging his shoulders, he turned the key and opened the door and the reason for the buzzing became immediately apparent. Flies, thousands of them, they were everywhere. Seated at the kitchen table was a vaguely human form that consisted of a black, writhing mass and the smell, Christ!

Well, this explained why the silly old bastard hadn't been to see them for a while. What the fuck was he going to do now? It was obviously too late to call an ambulance, but he supposed he should let the police or somebody else know. All at once a thought struck him. If this was the old bastard, then where was the old girl?

Step by stomach-churning step, he made his way through the kitchen and out into the hallway at the bottom of the stairs. If it were possible the density of flies increased with each step. By the time he'd reached the upstairs landing the buzzing in his ears was almost deafening. Quickly, he pushed open the door to the main bedroom. The scene downstairs had been bad enough, but this was like something out of the most graphic of horror films and the man quickly turned away and violently vomited the contents of his stomach. The figure that laid in the bed could no longer be described as human, if it ever had been. The man could stand it no longer and he bolted from the room, down the stairs, and out of the back door, through which he had entered a mere few minutes earlier. Once outside he collapsed to his knees and proceeded to take large gulps of cold, crisp, fresh air.

`Come on d'Artagnan...' he said out loud a few minutes later. `...this is no way for a musketeer to conduct himself. Pull yourself together man, you're as bad as those three spineless bastards downstairs.'

With that, he braced himself and re-entered the house. Desperately fighting the natural urge to vomit, now that his stomach was empty, he once again made his way through the kitchen and into the hallway. Snatching up the phone handset he quickly dialled nine, nine, nine.

`Hello? Yes, police please...'

Chapter 25.

Friday 20th January 2017, 1.00.p.m.

`Sorry to have kept you waiting. I'm Inspector Dennis, this is my colleague Sergeant Jacobs.'

`No problem Inspector, I haven't been here long. Tony North, Anthony West as was.' The man got up from his seat and shook hands with the two detectives.

Early-forties, medium height, deeply tanned, with long, sun-bleached hair. He was every inch the archetypal `surfer-boy' that Dennis had imagined he was going to meet.

`I hope you had a pleasant journey up here this morning Mr. North. Thanks for coming at such short notice by the way.'

`Everything went beautifully until we were about ten minutes from Doncaster station when we came to a complete standstill for an hour and a half. An incident on the line was the only explanation offered.'

`The great British transport system at its finest as usual.' Jacobs smiled.

`If only that were true Sergeant. It felt almost as if it took as long to get up here as it did to get back from Oz the other day.'

`Well, let's just hope that you haven't had a wasted journey. As Andy Gibbons explained to you on the phone, we're almost sure that the remains that have been found are those of your brother but we require a sample from your good self so that a DNA comparison can be carried out to confirm this.'

`And I'm more than happy to oblige Inspector. If the er... remains do prove to be Simons' how long will it be before I can give him a decent burial.'

`I'd have to check to be absolutely sure but I should think almost immediately. We have the cause and time of death so, I can't see any reason to delay funeral proceedings unnecessarily.'

`I appreciate that Inspector. I shouldn't think it'll be much of a service though. I'll just put him in with Mam and Dad, obviously it'll have to be a catholic service but I imagine there'll only be me there, I can't see that bitch in America lowering herself to come.'

`If you let us know when it's likely to be Mr. North, Jacobs and I will attend.'

`I certainly will Inspector. Is there any chance I could see him while I'm here?'

`I'll get Andy to take you over there now. In fact, we can kill two birds with one stone, Andy can organise your swab or whatever the procedure for DNA testing is these days at the same time. Do us a favour and give him a shout will you D.J?'

`No probs Boss.' Jacobs left the room.

`Well, thank you once again for taking the time Mr. North.' Dennis stood up and offered his hand.

`The least I could do Inspector. You'll keep me informed if there's anything I need to know, won't you?'

`Absolutely, ah here they are now. Andy, will you escort Mr. North to the mortuary to see the remains and see if you can organise the tests he came for?'

`Right yer are Sir. If you'd like to come this way Mr. North?'

`Thanks again, Inspector, Sergeant.' Tony North nodded to the two men and then followed D.C. Gibbons out of the office.

`The very epitome of the mid-life crisis don't you think D.J?'

`Oh, I don't know Troy, he's living the dream if yer ask me. Whatever he does for a living, spending half yer life surfing the waves knocks spots off what me an' you spend forty or fifty hours a week doing.'

`Well, I suppose when you put it like that. Why do I not find it surprising when an aging rocker finds an affinity with a forty-something surfer dude?'

`That's life I suppose Troy mi old mucker.'

`Anyway, it's almost two o' clock. I want you to go and pick Logan up, take him to see that old boss of yours.'

`Bill Quinn? What's Logan want wi' him?'

`Something he's found in those old papers. I don't know if it'll amount to anything but I'm inclined to trust his intuition. It shouldn't take you much more than a couple of hours. Pick me up here when you're finished and the three of us can call for a few pints up at the Hill Top, I quite like Friday evenings in there.'

`That's a cracking idea Troy, I quite fancy a few pints o' that porter they do up there, hope he's got it on this week.'

`Well, I'm sticking to lager. I only tried that porter once over Christmas, four pints and I could hardly lift my head off the pillow for two days!'

`Beats me how a fuckin lightweight like you ever made Inspector!'

`Correct me if I'm wrong D.J. but I don't recall any section of the Inspectors' exam that required you to be able to drink three-quarters of your own body weight and still be able to function.'

`Mebbe there ought to be then.'

`If that were the case D.J. you'd have been Assistant Chief Constable by now.'

`Only *Assistant*?' Jacobs laughed as he left the office.

Chapter 26

Friday 20th January 2017, 3.00 p.m.

`Well fuck me drunk, yer don't see a bloke for months on end and then up he pops twice in space of a few days. What can I do for yer D.J.?'

Bill Quinn put down his spanner, wiped his oily hands on the front of his overalls, and lovingly patted the petrol tank of the old motorcycle he'd been working on.

`Just wondering if yer could spare us half an hour of yer valuable time Sir. This is Logan Harvey, he's been helping us out by going through them old papers o' Cedric Shorts' and he's got a couple o' questions he thought you might be able to help him wi'.

`Pleased to meet yer Son, I hope this lot are paying yer for yer efforts?'

`Not a penny, I'm only too happy to help, it's made for some very interesting reading.'

`Very civic-minded of yer, fuck all help towards yer mortgage payments though.'

`That's one cross I'm lucky enough to never have had to bear, mi Grandad left me his house when he died.'

`Jammy bastard. Any road, let's get into house, D.J. can make himself a cup o' tea an' me an' thee can have a proper drink.'

****

`Reyt, what is it yer think I can help yer wi'?'

The old man asked a few minutes later. He and Logan were seated at the small coffee table, each with a can of lager in front of him. Jacobs was standing at the living room door, a large mug of tea in his hand.

`Go on Loge, I'll let you explain mate.'

`Right, I spent all morning, plus most of last night, going through everything yer gave to D.J. an' I've got to say that Cedric Short was a remarkable man...'

`He were a bit more than that son...' Quinn interrupted. `...he were the finest copper as ever carried a warrant card. Did yer know he never worked a murder case that he dint solve? Almost forty years on the force an' he never let a murderer slip through his fingers.'

`That's very impressive...'

`Impressive? It's fuckin well unheard-of son. I were always telling my teams how he had a clear-up rate that were second to none, weren't I D.J.?'

`Aye, I seem to recall as yer did mention it once or twice over years Sir.' Jacobs said deadpan from the door.

`Don't be a smart-arse Sergeant, nobody likes smart-arses.' Quinn smiled. `Any road, carry on young Logan an' I'll try not to interrupt again. Force of habit I'm afraid. When the wife's here I can't get a word in edgeways so, when I'm in other company I tend to have a fondness for the sound o' mi own voice.'

`Mrs. Quinn still away tree-hugging is she Sir?'

`Aye D.J., till tomorrow any road. She phoned this morning, so's I could give her a good listening to, an' fuck me she's gone an' got a bee in her bonnet about fracking in North Yorkshire now! God alone knows where it'll all end. Any road, you were saying Logan?'

`Right, I'm not even sure this is important or not but a couple of times, once in one of his diary entries and again in his last letter to you,

Cedric makes mention of his suspicions that Brian Sutton and a Chief Constable Baker were somehow in collusion...'

`Yer what? I've read them papers several times an' I don't recall seeing any o' that an' old Cedric certainly never mentioned to me that he thought that were case.'

`It's at the end of his letter...' Logan flicked through his notes. `... here it is. `... that bastard at Rampton and Ed Baker were thick as thieves...'

`Let me stop yer there son, I can see where yer going wrong. When old Cedric talked about `that bastard at Rampton' he weren't on about Brian Sutton, oh no, he were talking about...'

****

Chapter 27

Friday 20th January 2017, 3.45.p.m.

Troy Dennis was sitting at his desk, jacket removed, tie loosened, and shirt sleeves rolled-up past the elbows, contemplating recent events. He had just returned from a meeting with the Chief Constable, the result of which had left him until Wednesday to bring the whole Simon West affair to a satisfactory conclusion before it was consigned to the back-burner. `Far more pressing matters than a thirty-five-year-old inquiry Troy' she had said. In truth, he couldn't really argue the point. Despite recent findings, that seemed to suggest mistakes had been made all those years ago, what they were lacking was hard evidence and in any case, there was no suggestion of any wrong-doing on the part of the police. They had a signed, voluntary confession so, to all intents and purposes, all they really had was the missing body from a long ago solved murder case.

None of this sat easily with Dennis however. He hated knowing that the wrong man had been convicted and, ergo, the real killer had escaped justice but having no way to prove it.

Come on Denno, snap out of it. He thought to himself. You're going to end up like old Cedric what's-his-face if you're not careful, you can't possibly solve every case that comes across your desk. Anyway, you've got until Wednesday, three days, five if you count the weekend, for something to turn up. Maybe D.J. and Logan might get lucky.

`Got a minute Sir?'

D.C. Lisa Carter tapped on the open door and entered.

`Yes, what is it Lisa?'

`We've had a report of a couple of suspicious deaths at an address in Conisborough Sir. Looks like a husband and wife murder and suicide, both been dead for above a week by all accounts. Anyway, the reason I thought it might be of interest to us is the address. It's on Minneymoor Lane Sir, you know, the same place Simon West was found?'

`Mmm... could just be a coincidence Lisa but, as you know, I don't like coincidences.'

`That's not all Sir. You know Carol Cook in dispatch?'

Dennis nodded for her to continue.

`Well, it was Carol who passed it on to me and the recording of the original report is quite unusual. May I Sir?' Lisa indicated to the computer on Dennis' desk.

`Be my guest Lisa. You know I hate the bastard things.'

A few seconds of tapping on the keyboard followed before Lisa stepped back.

`Here we go Sir. I've skipped past most of it and gone straight to the interesting bit.'

From the computers' speaker came a rather high-pitched male voice.

`... it looks like the silly old bastard's gone and done himself in, the old dear as well. There's fuckin' flies everywhere an' all. When yer come don't forget to bring supplies. Me an' the boys need wine, beer and plenty of food. Oh, and don't forget the fags.'

The caller then hung-up.

`Well that's certainly unusual.' Dennis said now. `Meet me in the car-park in five minutes Lisa, you can drive, and we'll go and have a look. Do we have a name for the victims yet?'

`Yeah, a Henry Dutton and his wife Doreen, at least they're the house owners.'

`Henry Dutton you say? Where the hell have I heard that name recently?'

`Dunno Sir. It's not exactly a common name but it's hardly unusual either.'

`Never mind, it'll come to me. Right, chop, chop, Lisa. Car-park five minutes.'

`Already gone boss.'

D.C. Carter made a hasty exit.

`Dutton. Henry Dutton. Come on Troy, think man.' Dennis said to the empty office. `Fuck it!' he added, grabbing his jacket from the back of the chair and beating a hasty retreat of his own.

****

Twenty minutes later Dennis and D.C. Carter were just approaching the water tower at Conisborough when the opening bars of `Fog on the Tyne' resonated loudly within the confines of the car.

`It was my late-wifes' favourite song.' Dennis said, shrugging sadly as he reached into his jacket pocket for his mobile phone. `Hello Logan, what have you got for me?'

`I'm still not sure if this means anything but me an' D.J. are just leaving Bill Quinn's' house now. He's managed to clear up a couple of things, the main one being that Cedric Short was convinced that his old Chief Constable and the Head of Department at Rampton, some bloke called Dutton, who was in charge of Br...'

`Dutton you say? Henry Dutton?'

`Yeah, that's the feller. Anyway, it seems Cedric thought that him an' this Chief Constable Baker were up to no good back in the day...'

`Right, that settles it. I want you and D.J. to get your arses down to where young Wests' body was discovered the other week. I'll see you there, we're about five minutes away. I'll fill you both in when you get there. Bye now.'

Dennis cut the connection and placed his phone back in his pocket.

`I hope I'm not jumping the gun here Lisa but for the first time since this whole affair started, I get the feeling that we might actually be getting close to putting this one to bed. It's the next right pet, just after the bus-shelter.'

****

Chapter 28

Friday 20th January 2017, 5.00 p.m.

`Christ Almighty! It dunt half reek in here.' Jacobs said wrinkling his nose.

`You should have been here a couple of hours back, at least most of the flies have dispersed now.' Lydia Duncan replied from behind her face mask. ` There's a spare mask in there or a jar of Vicks if you'd prefer.' She pointed to her bag.

`Cheers Dusty.' Jacobs took a large finger full of vaporub and smeared it generously across his moustache. `Much better that. Is the boss about?'

`Him and D.C. Carter are upstairs with the other body. It smells even worse up there D.J.'

`Int life just a bowl o' cherries? Best go show mi face though. I'll catch yer in a bit love.'

`No need for that, I'm not planning on running… stud.' She said suggestively and winked.

`Dusty!' Jacobs hissed.

`What? Nobody else heard me.' She whispered back. `Don't worry yer sexy beast, that beard o' yours'll hide most of yer blushes.' She added.

`Reyt, err… I'd best be off then.' Jacobs said as he squeezed his bulky frame between the table and cooker in the small kitchen and made for the hallway, leaving Dusty laughing happily to herself.

****

Dusty was right. As bad as things were downstairs in the kitchen, they were nothing compared to the scene Jacobs found in the main bedroom. The smell alone seemed to have multiplied threefold and Jacobs was beginning to wish he had accepted the offer of a face mask. Unlike in the kitchen the flies here had obviously decided not to leave the party early. Troy Dennis and Lisa Carter were standing just outside the door watching as a team of technicians prepared to move what Jacobs assumed had once been a human being.

`Ah D.J., made it at last. Logan not with you?' Dennis' voice was muffled from behind his mask.

`Yeah, well, he got as far as the door anyway afore he decided as the smell were too much for him. He's waiting in car, listening to mi Rory Gallagher c.d. by the way.'

`Really? Well there's no accounting for taste I suppose but I must say I expected more from a man like him.'

`Nowt wrong wi a bit o' Rory Gallagher sir, bloody good guitarist he was.'

`I don't doubt it for a second Sergeant. Anyway, let's get a breath of fresh air ourselves. You can get off if you like Lisa, I'll get a lift with Jacobs, we only live a few minutes down the road.'

`Right you are Sir.'

`And Lisa?'

`Sir?'

`Go straight home, no popping back to the station to stare at a computer screen. It's Friday night for Gods' sake, a young girl like you should be out painting the town red.'

`I'm not so young Sir. I'm almost twenty-six.'

`Twenty-six eh? You hear that Sergeant? Still nowt but a bairn, is she?'

The three of them had by this time reached the front door and were standing in the porch.

`Aye, he's reyt lass. I've got kids older than you. In fact, come to think of it, I've probably got *socks* older than you.'

`The sad truth of it is Lisa, he's not joking. Now go home girl and enjoy your weekend.'

****

`Well boys, I'm eagerly awaiting your opinions.' Dennis said a few minutes later.

He, Jacobs, and Logan Harvey were sitting in Jacobs' car, with the windows wound up, the engine running, and the heaters on full blast in an attempt to take some of the chill out of the evening.

`Well, it seems to me that old Cedric may well have been onto something all along, exactly what is any fuckers guess though.' Jacobs said.

`I agree with D.J., this Henry Dutton bloke is connected to everything somehow. Any other explanation relies far too much on coincidence for my money.'

`We're all of the same mind then. I've always had an aversion to coincidence as well. So, what exactly did your old super have to say that was so interesting D.J.?

`I'll let Logan explain Troy, after all, it were him an' Bill as were doing most o' talking.'

`It's like I said to yer earlier Denno, something in those papers yer gave me to read through piqued my interest. On a couple of occasions old Cedric made mention of his old Chief Constable and `that bastard at Rampton'. I took this to mean that he thought his old boss and

Brian Sutton were somehow in collusion. Well, it turns out that `that bastard at Rampton' was none other than the late Henry Dutton who was in charge of Suttons' case when he was first committed in the eighties.'

`And whose body our esteemed pathologist Dusty currently prepares for removal. Anything else Loge?'

`Well, it seems that this Chief Constable Baker and Henry Dutton were often seen together at social engagements, yer know, charity fundraisers and the like and they often played a round of golf together. This is what led, according to Bill Quinn anyway, to Cedrics' conviction that the two of them were up to no good together. Apparently, he never actually voiced these concerns in public but relations between Cedric and Baker became somewhat frosty right up until Bakers' death.'

`I still don't see exactly what he was getting at. Did he think that Cedric and Baker were somehow responsible for Simon Wests' death or, was his fixation with the two of them something else entirely?'

`If we go back to the last letter he wrote to Bill Quinn...' Logan reached into his pocket and produced his note-book.`... there's a passage here that makes me think he thought they knew more about the young lads' murder than they were letting on. Here it is, `... there's been a cover-up on a monumental scale. While we're at it, watch your back where Eric Daltons' concerned as well, he's poison that one. He's also Ed Bakers' son-in-law so, he might have something to do with all this.'

`Eric Dalton eh? Another blast from the recent past and just like Cedric, Baker, and now Henry Dutton, no longer with us. It feels like we're getting closer but all those who could help prove any of these theories are dead and gone, in some cases have been for years.'

`Yer reyt though Troy, I get the feeling as we've got all the answers at our fingertips, summat'll turn up soon mate, it's got to.'

`I hope you're right D.J., I had a meeting with the Chief Constable earlier. She's given us until Wednesday to bring this whole sorry mess to a satisfactory conclusion.'

`Won't this class as new evidence, so to speak, so you might get an extension?' Logan asked.

`Strictly speaking, these new murders are not actually my case yet. We're only here because of the tenuous connections to young West. No, until further notice, this one's Geoff Harris' baby.'

`Speak of the devil an' he's sure to appear.' Jacobs nodded towards the windscreen and pressed the button that lowered the drivers-side window. `Ay up Bomber, how's it going pal?' he asked the tall man who now stooped down to the level of the window.'

`Not so bad D.J., yer looking well kid, yer Mam still feeding yer them pies is she.' D.I. Geoff `Bomber' Harris said smiling.

`Aye, she certainly is lad.' D.J. laughed and patted his belly.

`Ask her if she'll knock me up a couple o' steak an' ale when she gets a chance will yer big lad? I'll pay her o' course.'

`No probs mate.'

`Cheers Deano. You alright D.I. Dennis?'

`Fine thanks D.I. Harris and thanks for letting us have a look round.'

`Not a problem. I was actually hoping yer'd come to take over if I'm honest.'

`No, you're more than welcome to it. I'd appreciate it if you could keep me informed of any developments that might be of interest to our case though.'

`Will do. I've just come to let yer know I'm wrapping up for the evening. There's not much more as we can do tonight. The bodies are being loaded into meat wagon as we speak, then we're gonna lock her up tight an' start again in morning.'

`Yes, we're pretty much of the same mind. Couple of pints on the way home eh boys?'

`Sounds good to me where yer bound for?' Harris asked.

`We're just going to pop up to the Hill Top for a couple.'

`Aye, I know it. I'll just finish up here an' I'll meet yer there. Shall we say about twenty minutes?'

`I wouldn't be much longer, or you'll end up playing catch-up with the good sergeant here.'

`Oh, I wouldn't worry yourself too much on that score D.I. Dennis, wouldn't be the first time D.J. and me ave done a session together. See yer up there.'

****

Chapter 29

Friday 20th January 2017, 7.30 p.m.

York

Having spent a pleasant day shopping the ladies; Katie O'Hanlon, her daughters Eileen and Niamh, and Grace Morgan had enjoyed a delightful early evening meal in a small restaurant before Katie had loudly announced that it was `... high time we ladies got a feckin' good drink inside of ourselves'.

And so, the four women now found themselves sitting at a small table in one of the many hostelries that York had to offer, glasses fully charged and already more than a little the worse for wear. At a table just inside the door two middle-aged men were entertaining their small audience with a selection of easy-on-the-ear songs. Both were very accomplished guitarists and singers. The intimate nature of the venue and the relatively small gathering combined to create a comfortable environment in which to enjoy a few drinks. To this end the ladies had decided to stay where they were for the time being, rather than braving the cold January night in search of pastures new.

`Right, I've had about enough of that auld feckin' lager now. Niamh, it's your turn at the bar now, I'll have a vodka and cola. Come on girl the clocks against us.' Katie said suddenly.

`It's only half-nine Mam.' Niamh replied

`And sure, they'll be shouting last orders in another hour or so and I'm just getting the taste for it.'

`When was the last time you heard a last orders bell Mam?' Eileen asked now. `I don't think they even ring one in the Catholic Club any more. They certainly won't be ringing one in a city centre pub on a Friday night.'

`Are you sure about that now? Sure, they might just be waiting for the likes of us to leave before they start serving the regulars again.'

`I'm sure Mam, trust me on this one.'

`Right, well I'll take your word for it then so, but that doesn't change the fact that I'm sitting here with an empty glass in front of me. Come on Niamh get a move on girl.'

`Mam, that glass is still half-full for Christs' sake!' Niamh said exasperatedly.

`Ah, will you listen to my second-born Grace, always the optimist? Half-full is it? Watch... it's feckin well empty now. Now, get to the feckin bar like you've been told girl.' Katie slammed the now empty glass down on the table smiling.

`God, give me strength.' Niamh muttered as she got out of her seat.

Ten minutes later, with all glasses fully replenished, there was an announcement from one of the performers.

`Ladies and gents, it's time for our guest singer to get up and entertain us with a couple of Irish songs. Please welcome, for one night only, Eileen from Doncaster.'

There was a smattering of applause from the audience.

`Go on then girl, why are you still sitting there? go do your ting.'

`Mam! I swear, one of these days I'm going to fuckin' swing for you. When did you arrange this?'

`Sure, I just happened to bump into one o' them fine fellas on mi way back from the ladies and while I was congratulating him on his singing it just sort o' slipped out that my own daughter has the voice of an angel and she can play that auld guitar as well as himself. Anyways, away with you and go prove to him that your Mother's no liar.'

`One of these days... oh, balls to it!'

Eileen got out of her chair and made her way self-consciously to the front. A few moments of whispered conversation with the two men followed before she strapped one of the guitars over her shoulder and turned to the microphone. For the next twenty minutes a hush descended amongst those present. All conversation stopped and, apart from the occasional cough or sniffle the only sounds to be heard were Eileen's voice and her accompanying strumming on the borrowed guitar.

When, at last, she unslung the guitar, to rapturous applause from everyone, the landlord was heard to call loudly...

`That table drinks on the house for the rest of the night. Well done sweetheart, that was beautiful.'

Eileen made her way back to her seat, blushing furiously all the way.

`Oh well done Eileen love. See? I knew you'd do us proud.' Katie was still standing and applauding wildly as Eileen regained her seat.

`Nice one Big Sis.' Niamh said smiling.

`That really was amazing Eileen. What was that last song you sang? I've never heard anything like it in my life.' Grace added.

`It's called `The Galway Shawl' it's a personal favourite of mine.'

`Aw Jesus, do you remember when you sang that for your Granddad Danny the same night that he left us?'

`Yes Mam, it was shortly after that mi Uncle Pat taught me how to play the guitar and banjo.'

`And she's never looked back since, have you love?' Katie said smiling broadly.

`Whatever Mam. Can we talk about summat else now please?'

`Suit yourself but it's a rare talent you have there is all I'm saying. She gets it from her father you know Grace.'

`That's not altogether true Mam. Yer not a bad little singer yerself.' Niamh said.

`Well, I suppose you could say we're quite a musical family right enough. It's how I met the `Big Fella' after all.'

`Really? Tell me more.' Said Grace.

`It was the summer of sixty-six, England had just won the world cup and I was over here visiting friends. Anyway, all's anybody was talking about was the feckin football, enough to drive you mad it was, especially being Irish with the state of our national team. So, it was one Saturday night and Shirley, that's the friend I was over here visiting, and I decided to pop over to the Catholic Club to watch this auld Irish band that was doing the rounds back then. Well, for whatever reason the band cancelled at very short notice and the place was packed to the rafters with people waiting to see them play. Everybody was awful disappointed like. Anyway, after a while a few of the boys start singing amongst themselves, no music mind, just singing the songs from memory and bloody good some of them were as well. Well, the drink starts to flow, as it does, and everybody's getting a wee bit merry when, all of a sudden, Shirley nudges me and says in a loud voice `sing em The Black Velvet Band Katie lass.' Well I could have feckin died right there and then and I starts protesting an' telling her to shut the feck up and all that when suddenly, I hears this big, booming voice, `I'd like to hear that one lass, go on girl, give us a song'. I look around and standing there with a pint in one hand, a fag in the other, and a twinkle in his eye, is the most handsome man I ever saw in mi life. Tall and well-built he was, with a full head of jet black hair, and the most piercing blue eyes you ever did see. I found out later that night that he was hung like a feckin horse as well...'

`Mam!' Eileen and Niamh exclaimed in unison.

`What? Don't tell me you believe all that auld shite about every bride being a virgin on her wedding night in those days. Your father charmed the knickers off of me that very night, sure it might even have been the night you were conceived Eileen. We were married the following January and I carried you down the aisle with me girl. Fifty years it'll be this day next week.'

`Far too much information Mam.' Eileen said blushing furiously.

`Ah, get away with yourself, sex has always happened and always will. You might never have married but you've seen your fair share of bedroom ceilings yourself my girl and you Niamh, sure were you not pregnant yourself the day you married Logan?'

`That's as maybe Mam but there's no need to embarrass Grace like this.'

`Embarrassing Grace is it? It's the two of you I'm after embarrassing.' Cackled Katie. `Aw Jesus, the look on your faces but go on then I'll behave myself and spare your blushes.'

`A bit late for that now.' Eileen muttered.

`Did you sing `The Black Velvet Band' Katie?' Grace asked now.

`I did indeed, and I got a standing ovation from everyone there. Anyway, that's how I met the `Big Fella' and all this talk has made me awful thirsty. Your round I think Grace, I'll have a vodka and cola, you might as well make it a double girl, after all did the boss man not say they were on the house? It'd be a shame not to make the most of it.'

****

Chapter 30

Saturday 21st January, 3.00 a.m.

York

Eileen awoke in the hotel room she was sharing with Grace Morgan to an unfamiliar pressure on her chest.

`What the f...'

`Shush, be quiet. Eileen.'

`Grace, what the fuck are you playing at?'

`I said to be quiet or you're likely to get hurt!' Grace snapped as she switched the bedside lamp on.

In the dim light Eileen became fully aware of her predicament. Grace Morgan was straddling her chest and had a steak knife pressed to her throat.

`I don't want to hurt you Eileen, at least not just at the moment, but you and I need to have a little chat.'

`How the hell are we supposed to have a conversation when I've got a knife to mi neck?'

`You just lie there and listen to me, I'll let you know when I want you to answer, understand?' Grace pressed the knife harder into Eileen's skin, almost to the point of drawing blood.

With little other option Eileen just nodded mutely.

`Good. Now, I want to know all about this saint you knew as Uncle Pat, my real father, the man who deserted me and left me to the devices of that bastard. Tell me, when you were young, about six or maybe seven, did he ever come to your bedroom to read you a bedtime story? Well... did he?'

`Not very often no. Sometimes, if he happened to be at our house he'd tell us some of the old folk tales that Grandad Danny used to tell him when he was little.'

`Oh how sweet. And while he was telling you these lovely tales would he make you stroke *his* tail?'

`No of course not. Don't be dis...'

`And then, would he make you put it in your mouth while his big, thick, painful fingers invaded your most private places?'

`No, no, never. Why would you think...'

`Because that's what Saint Patrick abandoned me to!' Grace hissed angrily. `Three or four times a week, between the ages of six and nine, that bastard Eric Dalton, who I was brought up to call Daddy, would subject me to all manner of horrific things. While you, you and your bitch of a sister, get the love and affection that was mine by rights. You get to play the guitar while I was made to play the whore before I was even old enough to understand any of it.'

`You can't blame me or Niamh for any of that Grace.'

`But I *can* blame Pat O'Hanlon for deserting me and seeing as how he's no longer with us, you by association.'

`Grace, for Christs' sake, listen to yourself. God knows my heart goes out to you for what you've suffered but how can you possibly justify blaming me or Uncle Pat for what's happened?'

For the first time since her ordeal began Eileen felt a slight lessening of pressure on the knife at her throat.

`Listen to me Grace. Rest assured if Uncle Pat had had any idea what you were going through, he would have ripped Eric Dalton limb from limb with his bare hands. Quite possibly singing to himself while he did it.'

Suddenly, Graces' face crumpled. She threw the knife into the far corner of the room, rolled off Eileen, and curled up in a ball on the floor, sobbing hysterically.

Eileen, for her part, sat up gingerly and checked herself over. Finding no damage, apart from a slight soreness at her neck, she climbed from the bed and knelt before the prostrate form on the floor.

`Grace, Grace, come on stand-up girl.' She said gently.

`Oh Eileen, I'm so sorry.' Grace said between sobs.

`Come on sweetheart, stand-up, look at me.' Eileen helped the other woman to her feet and cradled her face gently in her hands. `Look at me Grace love.'

Eileen O'Hanlon was, by far, the most sweet and gentle natured of her whole family. As a child she had always been the one to nurse an injured bird back to health, or place a saucer of milk out for a hedgehog. As an adult she did more than her fair share of charity work and was a regular donor to causes such as The Red Cross and, her particular favourite, the RSPCA. She was also, however, the daughter of `Big Jud' O'Hanlon.

In one fluid movement, she brought her head back and swiftly forward again, administering a vicious head-butt to the bridge of Graces nose, the like of which any street-fighter worth his salt would have been proud. This was quickly followed by two back-handed slaps to the face, before she threw the now heavily bleeding Grace violently onto the bed.

`Right…' she said now `…It's your turn to listen to me and listen you will, if you know what's fuckin good for you. Like I said, I'm truly sorry for what happened to you while you were growing up but me and my family have done nothing but welcome you with open arms since we met you a fortnight since so, I don't know where you get off throwing that kindness back in our faces. Right, this is what's going to happen now. I'm going to mi Mam and Niamhs' room for the rest of the night, you stay here, tidy yourself up, and get some rest. The four of us can have a long talk in the morning. Got it?'

Grace nodded. `I think you've broken my nose.' She said from behind her hands.

`Here, let me see.'

Slowly, Grace lowered her hands from her face. Once again Eileen gently cradled the other woman's face in her hands and examined her closely.

`Mmm, I think you might be right.' She said thoughtfully.

In another lightning-fast manoeuvre, she took hold of Graces' nose in one hand and twisted it brutally. This elicited a scream from the other woman.

`Keep the noise down for fucks' sake, you'll wake the whole hotel. I've fixed it for you now, it shouldn't hurt as bad. Mind you, yer gonna have a right pair o' shiners in the morning.' Eileen laughed.

`I'm glad you think it's funny.' Grace winced.

`Yeah, well let that be a lesson to you. Never start a fight you're not either prepared or able to finish. Oh, and one more thing, the head-butt was off me, the two slaps were for our Niamh. There's only me can call mi sister a bitch and get away with it. See you in the morning.' Eileen smiled sweetly as she left the room.

Chapter 31

Saturday 21st January 2017 8.45 a.m.

Troy Dennis was rudely awoken by the familiar tones of `Fog on The Tyne'. Groaning he reached blindly for the bedside table in a forlorn attempt to shut off his phones insistent ringing. Cursing loudly, he forced himself out of bed, retrieved the object of his annoyance from his trouser pocket, and hit the answer button.

`D.I. Dennis.' He said wearily into the handset.

`Morning mi old son are we well?'

`Actually, I feel like shit but thanks for asking. Come to think of it, who the hell *is* asking?'

`Well, it's a good job I'm not easily offended. Yer spend most o' yer night wi' a bloke an' then he's forgotten all about yer in morning.'

`Oh, it's you Bomber. What can I do for you?'

`It's more a matter o' what *I* can do for *you* mi old cocker. How soon do yer think yer can be up at the scene o' crime?'

`What, the Hill Top?'

`Ha-ha, no.' laughed Bomber. `Although wi' the state we got in I know what yer mean. No mate, I'm up at Minneymoor Lane, summat interesting's just turned up, thought yer might like to see for yerself.'

`Give me ten minutes to grab a quick coffee, and D.J. and I will have a walk up, call it twenty minutes or so.'

`We can go one better than that. My Sergeant will be outside your house in ten. It's bastard freezing out, no point walking when yer can ride eh? Ouse Terrace weren't it?'

`Yes, that's r...'

`Ten minutes then, see yer in a bit.' The line went dead.

`How the hell can anybody be so bastard cheerful the morning after a night like we had last night?' he muttered to himself.

`Coffee's nearly ready Troy, Bombers' lads on his way.' Dean Jacobs' voice boomed cheerfully up the stairs from the kitchen.

`Fuck me another one.' He grumbled as he staggered into his clothes.

****

`Well yer weren't kidding old lad, yer *look* like shit an' all.' Geoff Harris laughed as Dennis, Jacobs, and D.S. Rob Shaw joined him in the kitchen of the house where the two bodies had been found the previous day.

`Enough of the frivolity if you don't mind please Inspector. I'm fairly sure I said this recently but I'm *definitely* sticking to lager from now on, I honestly can't handle those real ales.' Dennis answered.

`Aye, they're not for everybody reyt enough but D.J. were reyt, that porter's a cracking drop o' beer.'

`I honestly don't know how the two of you do it Bomber.'

`I'll let thi into a little secret old lad. Your problem is that yer've sobered-up, that's why yer feel rough. The secret to being a successful piss-artist is that yer must remain at least slightly inebriated at all times.' Bomber laughed again. `Any road, follow me let's show yer what we've got.'

The four men quickly made their way upstairs to one of the smaller bedrooms where they found a young technician sitting before an impressive array of computer monitors.

`Looks like the bridge o' the U.S.S. Enterprise. I wunt ave a clue where to start.' Jacobs stated.

`Oh it's not quite as sophisticated as it looks but it's certainly a cut above your average home computer system. Jamie Daniels, but everybody calls me Jack.' The young man spun round in his chair and offered his hand to the newcomers.

`This is D.I. Dennis and D.S. Jacobs, D.S. Shaw you've already met.' Bomber made the introductions. `Show us what yer've got so far would yer Jack?'

`No probs Inspector. I got here fairly early this morning to make a start on this lot.' He indicated the bank of monitors and keyboards. `I'll not bore you with all the technical jargon. But the first thing I came across was this.'

A couple of clicks of the computer mouse later and one of the monitors sprung into life.

`What we've got here gentlemen is footage from an indoor cctv system, the cameras to which are hidden very discreetly all about the house. This particular example coincides with the time of the emergency call yesterday.'

After a few seconds of nothing happening a tall, slightly stooped figure could be seen entering the kitchen through the back door. After pausing for a while at the corpse at the kitchen table, the figure made its way from the room. The image on the screen flickered momentarily before being replaced by footage of the same figure climbing the stairs and entering the master bedroom. Another few moments passed before the man could be seen running from the bedroom, almost falling down the stairs in his haste. More flickering on the screen before the detectives got a brief view of the same man darting out of the kitchen door.

Jack fast-forwarded the footage and restarted it as the man re-entered the house. On the screen the figure marched through the kitchen and into the hallway. More flickering and then the man could be seen standing at the small telephone table with the phones' receiver pressed to his ear. A moment later Jack halted the footage.

`The only room in the house, as far as we've been able to ascertain, not covered by any cameras is the master bedroom.' He said now.

`Well, seeing as we already know what he found in there I don't see as that hinders us too much.' Bomber said.

`How far back does the footage go?' Dennis asked.

`The systems set to erase and re-record on a weekly basis. However, just before you arrived I found a file that looks as if it could contain saved recordings. I was just about to try and access it when I heard you coming up the stairs.'

`Well, what tha waiting for lad? Let's ave a gander.' Geoff Harris boomed.

After a few moments of furiously tapping at the keyboard and manoeuvring the computer mouse Jack sat back in his chair.

`Here we go gents, any particular date you'd like to see first. It looks like these recordings go back as far as two-thousand-and-nine.'

`Inspector?' Harris asked Dennis.

`Oh, I don't know. How about we go back a month and see from there? Can we just fast-forward through it until something interesting catches the eye though?'

`No problem Inspector.' Jack replied happily.

For the next ten minutes the five men watched the film before them as it scrolled quickly across the screen, occasionally one of them asking for the footage to be paused at a point of possible interest.

`I take it that's our man Dutton?' Dennis had said at one point when a small, balding, bespectacled man had appeared wandering from room to room.

`I'd say yer could take that to the bank Sir.' Jacobs had agreed.

After a few more minutes with nothing to see but the same elderly man going about his business Bomber broke the silence once more.

`How's about we run it forward to a week afore we found the bodies see if owt a bit more interesting crops up?'

`Sounds good to me.' Dennis agreed.

`Right-ho.' Jack said reaching once more for the controls.

`Hold yer horses young Jack.' Jacobs said suddenly.

`What is it D.J.?' Dennis asked eagerly.

`Not reyt sure Sir. Just roll it back a bit to where we see the old man wheeling that trolley will yer Jack?'

`O.K. Sarge.' Jack did as he was asked.

On the screen the old man could be seen pushing a laden supermarket trolley from the front door, down the hallway, and past the telephone table, before disappearing from view.

`Go forward a bit now son.' Jacobs said. `Reyt, back a bit... that's it, start again there.'

The old man could now be seen pushing the now empty trolley back to the front door and leaving the house.

`O.K. that'll do.' Jacobs said.

`What's yer point D.J.?' Bomber asked.

`Where did he go?' Jacobs replied.

`What do you mean D.J.?' Dennis joined in now.

`Exactly what I said. *Where* did he go?'

`Well, I suppose he went to put his shopping away.' Rob Shaw said now.

`Where?'

`The kitchen I'd imagine. Where do you normally put your shopping?'

`So why dint he trigger the camera in there then?'

`Where are you going with this D.J.?' Dennis asked.

`Well Sir, according to young Jack here, the only room in the house that int covered by a camera is the main bedroom, right Jack?'

The young technician nodded.

`So, we see our man come in the front door, walk down the hall as far as the bottom o' stairs an' then nowt for what ten minutes or so? If he'd gone into any o' downstairs rooms or kitchen he'd o' triggered one o' cameras covering them rooms wunt he? So, where the fuck did he get to?'

`Well, fuck my old pit cat!' Bomber blurted out. `He's got to ave been somewhere. Robbie, get every available body searching this house wi' a fine-tooth-comb, that bastard dint just vanish into thin air, there must be some sort o' hidden room or summat. Snap to it lad for fucks sake!'

As D.S. Shaw hastily made his way to do his superiors' bidding Dennis slapped Jacobs heartily on the back.

`Brilliant D.J.!'

`Aye, yer've got eyes like a shit house rat an' no mistake.' Agreed Harris. `Come on, let's get down there an' give em a hand.'

****

It didn't take long. Within a matter of minutes, the four detectives were standing in front of a heavy steel door that had been hidden behind what had at first appeared to be an old-fashioned Welsh Dresser, just to the right of the kitchen doorway. Upon closer examination, however, the dresser had turned out to be little more than a shell that swung easily out from the wall on well maintained hinges to reveal the hidden door.

`More bastard technology.' Bomber moaned upon seeing the digital combination pad at the side of the door. `Robbie, get young Jack down here sharpish, will yer lad?'

A few moments later the young technician was busily examining the touchpad and door.

`Obviously it'd be a lot easier if I had the combination, but I shouldn't think I'll have too much trouble overriding the system. Probably take me about ten or twenty minutes to gain access.'

`Reyt, I need a fag an' a breath o' fresh air any road, if that's not too much of a contradiction in terms. Give us a shout when yer've cracked it lad.' Bomber said making his way to the front door.

****

`Bingo!' Jamie `Jack' Daniels exclaimed fifteen minutes later. `Sir, we're in!' He shouted as he jumped up from his seat and raced for the stairs.

By the time he'd safely negotiated the staircase the four policemen were already waiting at the hidden door.

Jack pressed a key on the control pad and the heavy steel door slid open silently to reveal a short, well-lit staircase leading down to what could only be a basement of some description.

`Well, what are we waiting for? Let's see what all the secrecy's about then.' Bomber declared.

Slowly, the five of them descended the stairs, turning right at the bottom and finding themselves in a large, subterranean room.

`Well, it's about fuckin time! I hope you bastards have brought the supplies.' The tall, stooped man they had last seen on the computer monitors rose from his seat at the large table that was situated in the centre of the room.

'Oh, sweet suffering Christ. What the fuck is this place?' Jacobs' voice faltered.

The scene before them was like something out of the worst of nightmares.

Chapter 32

`Allow me to introduce myself. I'm D'Artagnan and these are my three companions Porthos, Athos, and Aramis.' The man bowed low and, with a sweeping gesture of his arm, indicated the table.

Seated around the table were the skeletal remains of what appeared to be three children. Each was secured to a chair, bound at wrists and ankles with large cable ties, their skulls grinning maniacally at those present. The ragged remnants of clothes clung to each skeleton and before each lay a plate of decaying food and a dusty glass of what may have been red wine.

`Just what the fuck have you done you fuckin animal?' Robbie Shaw launched himself forward, grabbing the man by his shirt, and forcing him up against the wall.

`N-n-nothing, I ant done nothing.' The man stammered.

`Sergeant! Get yer hands off him.' Geoff Harris barked.

`Get off him? I'm gonna fuckin kill him!' snarled Shaw.

`That's an order Robbie.'

Reluctantly, Robbie Shaw violently shoved the man away from him and retreated to the opposite corner visibly shaking with rage.

Troy Dennis approached the man who was now sitting with his back to the wall.

`What's your name mate? And I mean your real name, forget all the Three Musketeers shit.'

`D-D-Derek, Derek Dutton.'

`Right then Derek. Do you mind telling me what's been going on here? What the hell happened to these children?'

`I dint do anything to them.' Derek whined. `They're my friends.'

`Who did then Derek? Who hurt your friends?'

`The bad men. The policeman, the council man, and the teacher man and their friends.'

`When was this Derek?'

`A long time ago. We're safe now though, I look after us all now. Well, at least I do when the `Old Bastard' remembers to bring the supplies. He won't be coming any more though, he's dead, the `Old Dear' as well. I phoned for the police though, they might be here soon.'

`Yes, I know Derek, we're the police, me and my friends here. Now Derek, these `Bad Men' that you mentioned, can you remember any of their names?'

`I'm gonna make you squeal you little bastard, Uncle Eddie's gonna make you fucking squeal.' Derek's eyes had taken a far-off, haunted look as he uttered these last words.

`Eddie? One of the bad men was called Eddie?' Dennis asked gently.

`Yes, he was the `Bad Policeman'.'

`Can you remember any of the other men's names?'

`No, just him. E-Eddie. He was the worst. H-he used to smack us round the head, or reach round and squeeze our balls hard while he was sticking his thing in us.'

`How old were you when Eddie and his friends used to do this to you.'

`N-nine. They stopped doing it to me when I was twelve. Eddie said he didn't like hairy boys. `Young meat tastes the sweetest Henry my old friend.' The haunted look was back as Derek remembered these words. `That's when the other boys started coming.'

`What other boys Derek?'

`Younger boys, young meat for the `Bad Men'

`How many boys Derek?'

`Loads of em. Some only came once, others came a few times. Some never left.' He whispered quietly, looking forlornly at the table.

`Derek, do you have any idea what your friends' real names are?'

`Porthos is really called Peter, Athos is called Andrew, and Aramis is called Aaron. All our names begin with the same first letter as the musketeers, so I changed them for us.'

`And how long have the boys been here Derek?'

`I don't know exactly. Porthos was first, he came when I was eleven, I think. Then it was Athos, he came about a year later. Aramis came to stay on my sixteenth birthday.'

`And how old are you now Derek?' Dennis asked.

`I don't know exactly. I remember having my thirtieth birthday but that was a long time ago now. I might be forty or even older.'

`What year were you born Derek, do you know?'

` Oh yes, the twentieth of July nineteen-sixty-six.'

`Derek, that means that you're *fifty*-years-old.'

`Really? Well, fuck me drunk, did you hear that boys? If I'd known that we could have had a party.' He said to the table.

`Are you absolutely sure that Aaron or Aramis, whatever you call him, has been here since your sixteenth birthday?'

`Oh yes, that I know for certain. That was the day the `Old Bastard' said that I had to live in this room instead of the house. It was the same day that I saved the boy.'

`Saved the boy? What boy are you talking about?'

`The boy on the field, Simon I think his name was. He lived over on the Bradley Estate.'

Chapter 33

Tuesday 20th July 1982 9.45 a.m.

What the fuck was he still doing here? The bad men didn't normally stay overnight but there he was large-as-life `Eddie the Cunt' talking happily with the `Old Bastard'.

Derek Dutton crept closer in an attempt to hear what was being said.

`You really are going to have to reign it in a bit Ed.' Henry Dutton was saying. `That's the third death now. None of this was in the plan.'

`Plan? What fucking plan?' Chief Constable Edward Baker spat angrily. `Just remember, this was all as much your idea as mine. You provide the premises, the boys and I get our jollies, so to speak, and you get to do your precious research. Everybody's happy.'

`There was no mention of murder, or the covering-up thereof, at any point. As if you and your cronies aren't twisted enough without resorting to killing the poor bastards.'

`And what sort of moral high ground do you profess to take? You, a man who quite willingly offered the arse of his only child to be repeatedly buggered by myself and my cronies, as you so eloquently put it. Get a grip Henry, you've already got two stiffs down there, one more is hardly going to make a difference. If it makes you feel any better, I'll have a word with Roger and Charles, try and get them to curb their enthusiasm a little.'

`No more deaths Ed, I mean it. Any more and I'll shut the whole thing down.'

`Don't you dare threaten me you little shit! We go on until *I* say different, understand?' Baker grabbed the smaller man roughly by the shirt front.

`I'm not frightened of you Ed.' Dutton said meekly.

`Oh, but we both know different don't we Henry?' Suddenly Bakers' eyes narrowed as he stared out onto the field across the little lane. `Anyway, I think I'll smoke a cigar while I take a couple of laps of the field, then I'll be off. I'll see you on Friday as usual and let's have no more of this foolish talk. Good bye Henry.'

****

Edward Baker had spotted the slight figure of Simon West atop his perch on the `Kings Seat' quite by chance. Even from that distance, however, it was clear to his practised eye that the boy was just his type and he'd felt the old familiar stirring in his loins. Last nights' fiasco had left him feeling somewhat frustrated, he really was going to have to have a word with Roger about his and Charles' penchant for choking. Thus, he'd made up some story about taking a walk round the field whilst he had a smoke. Upon leaving his host he had made his way directly across the field to the patch of overgrowth that partially hid the rock upon which the boy was sitting. He timed his arrival perfectly. As he cleared the tree cover the boy was standing at the base of the rock with his back to Baker. Three quick paces covered the short distance between them. He grabbed the boy from behind, simultaneously pulling his t-shirt over his head, and forcing his face into the rock.

`I'm going to make you squeal yer little bastard!' he hissed into Simon Wests' ear, viciously tearing at the boys' clothes as he struggled with his own zipper.

****

Derek Dutton had carefully tracked Bakers' progress across the field and noted the exact spot at which he had left the open field for the cover of the overgrowth. Having been brought up here for all of his sixteen years he knew every inch of the `Minneymoor' intimately. To this end he slowly made his way via a much more circuitous route than that which Baker had taken, until he was mere feet away from the point at which the policeman had entered the bushes. After waiting for what seemed like hours to him, but in reality, couldn't have been much more than thirty minutes or so, curiosity got the better of him. Silently, he crawled through the long grass, ignoring the prickle of low-lying thistles, and desperately trying to avoid any nettles. For once `Lady Luck' was on his side. He had almost reached the small clearing at the foot of the `Kings Seat' when a movement caught his eye and brought him up short.

Baker, sweating profusely, and obviously out of breath, was struggling to his feet whilst trying to tuck his now flaccid penis back into his trousers.

Derek willed himself to become invisible. He closed his eyes tightly and clenched his fingers and toes. It was then that his hand curled around a rough, slightly sharp, object. Slowly opening one eye and being careful not to make any move that might alert Baker to his presence, he looked down to his right. There, nestled in the grass, was a chunk of limestone, similar to the ones he'd seen the other kids use as goalposts on the field in bye-gone days. I could easily cave that bastards head in with this, he thought now, no more `Eddie the Cunt'. Bracing himself, he lifted the rock and made his move.

****

Chapter 34

Saturday 21st January 2017 10.25 a.m.

`But I froze, by the time I was able to move again it was too late, Baker would've been halfway across the field. So, I went over to where the boy was lying. At first, I thought he were dead. He were laid on his front, all o' his clothes had been taken off an' there were a lot o' blood round his head an' scratches an' marks on his back an' his arse. Any road, I put mi hand on his shoulder, reyt gentle I were, an' that's when he moaned an' turned his head an' looked at me. That's when I saw it.'

`Saw what? What did you see Derek?' Dennis asked quietly.

`The look Mister Policeman, it was the look that I saw. The same look as I'd seen on all those boys faces for years, the same look as must o' bin on my face all them hundreds o' times as them bastards used mi to do whatever they wanted.'

`What look are you talking about Derek?' Dennis asked this last with a sense of dread and foreboding.

`It's the look that says `I want to die, please do something, don't let them do this to me anymore'. It's just one look but it says all those things at once. Have you ever seen a look like that Mister Policeman?'

For one dreadful moment, a vision of his late wife towards the end of her battle with cancer came into Dennis' mind but he shook his head.

`No Derek, I can't say that I have. What happened then?'

`That's when I saved him. I picked up the rock again and I did to him what I'd meant to do to `Eddie the Cunt'. I know you think I hurt him, that's what the `Old Bastard' always said an' all, but I really didn't, I really did save him.'

`Let me get this straight Derek. Are you saying that *you* killed Simon West?'

`Y-yes, I s-suppose I am, but he might have died anyway. Like I said, there was a lot o' blood but I made sure them bastards could never get their hands on him again dint I? Please Mister Policeman, yer've got to believe me I weren't trying to hurt him, I were just trying to make things better.' As he said this last, Derek grabbed at Dennis' arm imploringly.

`Calm down Derek.' Dennis said kindly. `I believe you.'

At this point Jacobs walked over and whispered something in his ear. Dennis nodded and turned back to Derek, who was now sobbing quietly.

`Derek, do you know what happened to Simons' hands?'

`W-what?'

`Did you do anything to Simons' hands?'

`Oh, that. It was to stop him from hurting anybody else.' Derek said matter-of-factly.

`I'm sorry, I don't understand.'

`I remember reading a long time ago that boys like us, as had to put up with all this shit, do the same thing to other young boys when they get older. So, whenever they die I break their hands to make sure that they can't hurt anybody else in another life. I did the same to those three.' Again, he gestured to the table. `Any road, after I'd seen to his hands I picked up his clothes and made mi way back home, I were gonna take em to police see, tell em everything I knew, but I were only just coming out o' bushes when I saw the `Old Bastard' standing down by gate so, I dashed o'er to other side o' field and hid the clothes under a tree near `Table Rock'. Then I went down an' met up wi' the `Old Bastard'.'

`And you've been locked-up in here ever since?'

Derek nodded. `I were all covered in blood. He beat the shit out o' mi 'til I told him what happened, made me show him where the boy was. I thought he might've fetched him back here, but he must've just left him out there, or done summat else wi' him. He said I'd fucked everything up an' that for mi own good I'd have to live down here with all the other boys as had fucked things up for him.'

`How did you manage to get out of here and phone for the police Derek?'

`There's a ventilation shaft back there as leads up to back garden, the cover on it came loose years ago. I used to sneak out to see the `Old Dear' sometimes, but it's harder to get through since I got bigger. I only went out last time cos we were running out o' stuff. That's when I found them and phoned for help.'

`Why did you come back here Derek? Why not wait at the house, or outside in the garden?'

`Cos this is where I belong. If anybody saw me I'd fuck everything up again, `Best for all concerned this way Derek. Damage limitation, that's the name of the game my boy.' This last was said in what the policemen assumed was an impersonation of his father/gaoler.

`Well we're going to get you out of here Derek, you're safe now. Don't worry we'll come back for your friends.' Dennis added when he saw Derek's panicked glance towards the table.

`Will I get into a lot of trouble for saving the boy Mister Policeman?'

`I shouldn't think so Derek. Come on, let's get you upstairs and then some friends of ours will take you to get something to eat eh?'

Derek nodded meekly and allowed himself to be led up and out of the prison he had called home for almost thirty-five years.

****

`So, what do yer make o' that lot then? Reminds me o' that bloke out in Austria or Finland a few years back. Pretzel or summat his name were.' Bomber Harris asked a few minutes later.

`Fritzl, his name was Josef Fritzl, but I know what you mean, there are striking similarities. If anything, I think this is a far more disturbing state of affairs though.' Dennis said.

The detectives were outside watching as the police car containing Derek Dutton carefully navigated its way up the pot-holed lane.

`Well it makes me sick to mi stomach.' Jacobs said now. `What kind o' sick bastard stands by an' watches as his own flesh an' blood is used an' abused like that?'

`I agree D.J., it's sickening. It's the first time I've ever solved a case and felt no sense of achievement. To be honest, I feel almost tainted, dirty in some way.' Troy Dennis looked at his friend and colleague, his face a picture of revulsion.

`Well, on that note mi old cocker, I hereby officially hand this case over to you Inspector Dennis. I'm sure yer'll agree, it ties in nicely wi' what yer've been working on. Let me get back to busting druggies an' other low-life.'

`Well, thank *you* Inspector Harris, you're all heart.' Dennis replied.

`The pleasure's all mine believe me. Be seeing yer.'

Geoff Harris saluted smartly and made his way to the car where his Sergeant was waiting.

`I hope you haven't made too many plans for what's left of the weekend D.J., looks like we're going to have our hands full.'

`Nowt as can't be altered Sir, at least the Chief Constable will be pleased, she gave us 'til Wednesday to wrap up dint she?'

`Yes D.J., she did, but something tells me that pleased will be the last way to describe her mood when she learns about this little lot.'

EPILOGUE

Friday 17th February 2017 4.40.p.m.

Town Moor Golf Club, Doncaster

Dean Jacobs made his way through the clubhouse and out onto the patio overlooking the eighteenth green. A lone figure was standing with his back to Jacobs, who could smell the smoke from the mans' cigar as he approached.

`Evening sir, everything alreyt?' He asked pleasantly.

`Ay up D.J., I'm sound lad. Just having mesen a smoke an' remembering old times. How's yerself?' Detective Superintendent (retired) Bill Quinn turned to face his former colleague smiling warmly.

`Knackered, if truth be known, but I'll get o'er it.'

`Aye, I daresay as yer are, yer've had yerself a busy few weeks by all accounts.'

`That's an understatement, but I think the worst of its behind us now.'

`Dunt speak too soon lad, tha's opened a reyt can o' worms wi' this little lot. Any road, what did yer want to see me about.'

`Bit of a courtesy call really. Troy, that's my boss, suggested I meet wi' yer an' fill yer in on a few things, seeing as yer had a bit of a vested interest, so to speak.'

`A bit more than that wunt yer say lad?'

`Aye, well that's as maybe but owt I tell yer has got to be in the strictest confidence Sir. We could both end up in a whole heap o' shit if anybody got wind o' this.'

`That goes wi'out saying D.J., an' cut the Sir shit, mi name's Bill, we've known each other long enough an' any road, it's a long time since I were yer boss.'

`Like you used to do wi' old Cedric yer mean Sir?'

`Aye tha's got a point there lad.' Bill Quinn laughed. `C'mon, let's get inside an' I'll buy yer a drink, yer off duty now aren't yer?'

`O.K., but just the one eh Boss, I'm in the motor?'

Ten minutes later the two old friends were sitting at a quiet table, each with a pint in front of him.

`The shit's really gonna hit the fan big time in the next few weeks, as if it ant already.' D.J. was saying. `We've been able to identify more than a dozen men, apart from Ed Baker, who were regular visitors to Dutton's little torture chamber between seventy-five an' eighty-four. It's a hell of a list Sir. Two more high-ranking coppers, several local councillors, a member of the clergy, a school teacher, and a minor league footballer are the ones I can remember off top o' mi head. Six men have also come forward to say as they were abused as youngsters in that basement, god knows how many more are out there.'

`It's Jimmy Saville all over again. How many are still alive to face the music?'

`One Sir, the footballer an' he's in a home suffering from late stages dementia. It sticks in mi craw, but these bastards are all gonna get away wi' what they did, while that poor bastard as were kept prisoner all them years spends his life locked away in some institution or other.'

`Aye, it's a bastard of a job we chose lad an' I'll tell yer summat else an' all. There'll be them still out there as won't thank yer for bringing all o' this to the fore, them as might not have taken part in any o' the less savoury aspects but will o' played a hand in covering it all up. Yer'll have to stay strong Deano an' just prove to everybody that for every bent copper as comes to light during yer investigation there's a dozen more, like me an' thee, an' that gaffer o' thine, an old Cedric o' course, who do this job for the right reasons an' can't an' won't be corrupted.'

`At least we finally proved old Cedric reyt though, dint we Sir?'

`*You* did D.J., you an' that Inspector o' yours an' for that I shall always be grateful. It's why I asked yer to meet me here. I wanted to tell him mesen as he'd finally bin vindicated after all them years.'

`Why here then Sir?'

`Cos he's out there, where yer found mi standing when yer first came in.' Quinn nodded towards the eighteenth. `We scattered his and his wifes' ashes on the eighteenth green a few years back, me an' his boys did. Got special permission off the club to do it. Did I ever tell yer D.J., he were the finest copper I ever worked wi'? He had a clear-up rate second to none.'

`Aye Sir, I think yer mebbe mentioned it once.' Jacobs smiled.

THE END

ACKNOWLEDGEMENTS

I found the latter stages of this book very difficult to write. The Truth in The Bones was not originally intended to be a story about child abuse, historical or otherwise, and I have been to places in my mind to which I have no desire to ever return (think I'll just stick to good old-fashioned murder in any future offerings!). Once I had started down that road however, I quickly realised there was no way in which to sugar coat the subject matter and the result is a much darker tale than I anticipated when I started writing way back in May. I sincerely hope I have not trivialised in any way this most heinous of crimes.

Similarly, the opening chapter of this book may to some readers appear crude, vulgar, or quite possibly offensive. It was never my intention to offend. I needed a valid reason for an eleven-year-old boy to be alone in the bushes on a summers morning. It is also an accurate representation of how yours truly first learned of the birds and the bees, I was nine-years old!!

Right, that's the conscience cleared, on with the thank yous.

First of all, to the woman without who none of this would have been possible, my beautiful wife Linda. The words are all mine, but you are my inspiration, and I love you dearly.

To our youngest daughter Beth, who was more than a little perturbed at not getting her picture in the first book, even though she neither bought nor read it! And who asked, nay demanded, to feature in this one, even going as far as to volunteer to be anything from a murderer to a bitch. I'm happy to say that she's neither. She is however the Hill Top barmaid who features in one of the early chapters. Maybe she might even buy this one!

Next to a man that I have never met Detective Inspector Peter Hoyland (retired), who provided me with invaluable assistance and information on matters pertaining to police procedures, promotions etc. Perhaps one day we two shall meet and share a pint or three.

To Paul `Ballo' Ballington who kindly agreed to feature, albeit fleetingly in chapter thirteen, of my little offering. If you've never listened to this lad I urge you to do so. He's very talented and very, very funny. I wish you all the best in the future mate.

To all my friends and family in The Hill Top, Conisborough who have been with me every step of the way and provided endless support and encouragement, not to mention copious amounts of alcohol! My heartfelt thanks. As with the aforementioned Mister Ballington, if you have never experienced the delights of this most welcoming of alehouses, I strongly advise you to do so, you won't be disappointed. If I happen to be in don't hesitate to come up and say hello. I don't bite, and it would be nice to meet some of the folk who have taken the time read my work and to thank you in person for all the messages of support, they really do mean a lot to me.

That's it, as before I really would appreciate any feedback/criticism. You can find me on Facebook or contact me via e-mail at

Thefeg.mf@gmail.com

Thank you all once again.

Mick Fenlon 23rd December 2017.

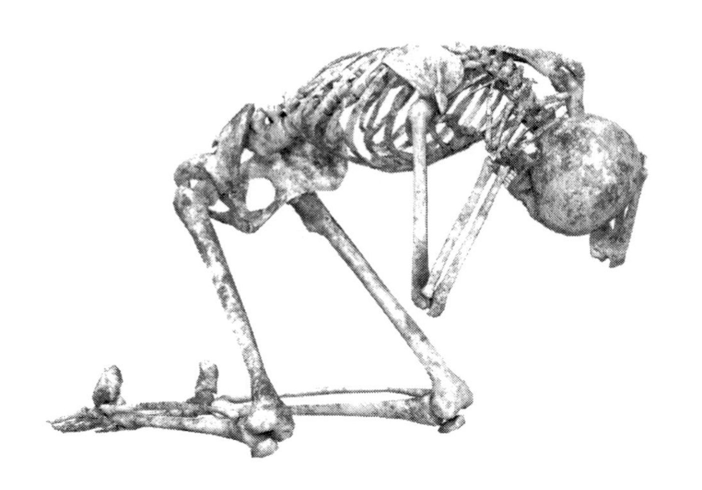

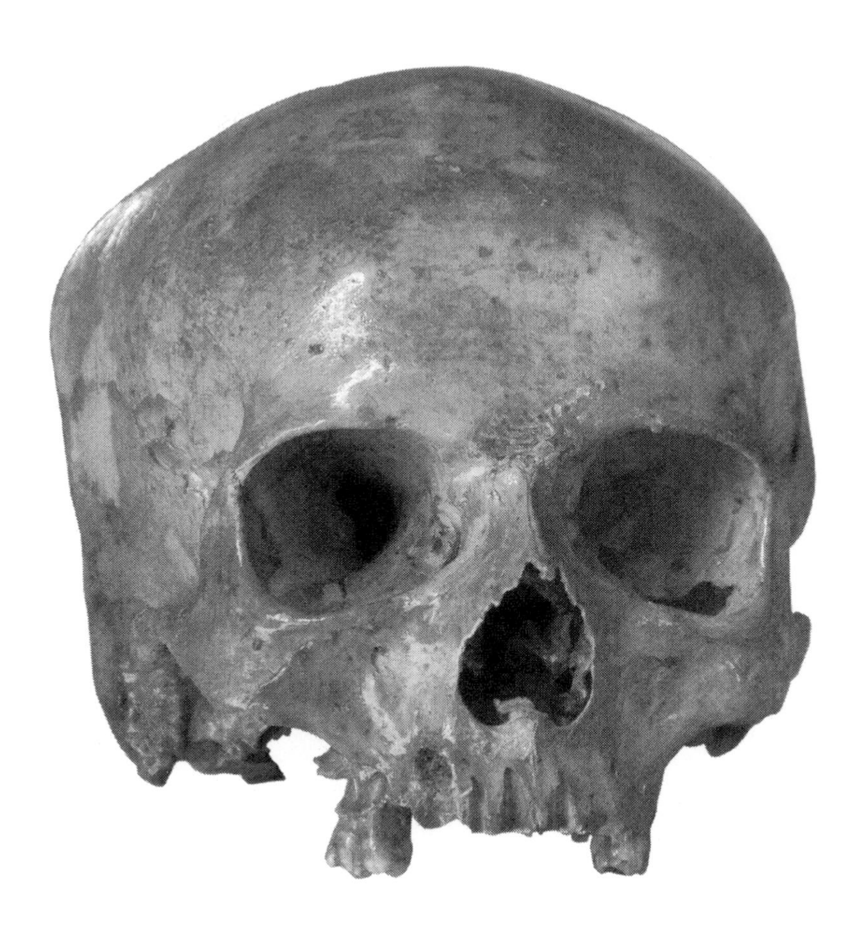